Don LePan
Animals

Don LePan is the founder of Broadview Press, an independent academic publishing house, and the author of several nonfiction books. This is his first novel. Born in Washington, D.C., he has lived in Canada for most of his life.

PRAISE FOR
ANIMALS

"A brave and frequently fascinating novel, wrought with painful choices, harrowing journeys, and a deep passion for its subject matter." —*Montreal Review of Books*

"Immediately gripping and deeply moving . . . this powerful tale . . . compels us to consider our own relationship to the fellow creatures that we love, abuse, and eat. *Animals* is an engrossing, elegantly written, and timely contribution to the great tradition of dystopic fiction." —Kathryn Shevelow, author of *For the Love of Animals*

"When Margaret Atwood wrote *The Handmaid's Tale*, she didn't take kindly to the label of science fiction, eventually telling the *Guardian*, 'Science fiction has monsters and spaceships; speculative fiction could really happen.' Apply her definitions to fellow Canadian Don LePan's first novel, and it becomes clear why *Animals* is so disturbing: the monsters are all-too-recognizably human. *Animals* depicts a terrifying future not too many generations down the road." —*The Montreal Gazette*

"Devastating. *Animals* is a powerful novel, and a fully convincing one." —P.K. Page

"Well-written and engrossing." —Angus Taylor, author of *Animals and Ethics*

"Provocative, original, beautifully crafted and achingly human, this is a novel that illuminates what we so called 'higher beings' strive to keep darkly hidden from our consciousness . . . *Animals* . . . is destined to become a classic." —Catherine Banks, author of *Bone Cage*

"A deeply moving narrative that can change your life—it did mine." —Thomas Hurka, author of *The Best Things in Life: A Guide to What Really Matters*

ANIMALS

ANIMALS

a novel

Don LePan

Originally published in Canada in 2009 by Véhicule Press
First American edition, 2010

Library of Congress Cataloging-in-Publication Data

LePan, Don, 1954-
Animals : a novel / Don LePan.
p. cm.
ISBN-13: 978-1-59376-277-3
ISBN-10: 1-59376-277-1
1. Environmental degradation—Fiction. 2. Extinction (Biology)—
Fiction. 3. Regression (Civilization)—Fiction. 4. Racially mixed
people—Fiction. 5. Food supply—Fiction. 6. Food—Moral and
ethical aspects—Fiction. I. Title.
PR9199.4.L463A55 2010
813'.6—dc22
2010010906

First American Edition

Cover design by Lynn Buckley
Interior design by Neuwirth & Associates
Printed in the United States of America

Soft Skull Press
An Imprint of Counterpoint LLC
2117 Fourth Street
Suite D
Berkeley, CA 94710

www.softskull.com
www.counterpointpress.com

Distributed by Publishers Group West

To Dominic and Naomi

Editors' Note

The background on how the Okun and Clark manuscripts together came into the publisher's hands is now a matter of public record, as are formal assurances from the publisher as to the appropriate permissions being in place to authorize the combined manuscript being made available to the public at large.

Clark's advisory from some years ago to the audience he was then addressing ("unless and until Professor Okun decides that she would like to take the further step of publishing the manuscript during her own lifetime, it must remain a private manuscript to which you have been permitted access in this context") is, of course, superseded.

The newspaper article quoted by Broderick Clark in these pages has now been identified as being a column by an American-Canadian journalist, Margaret Wente, entitled "Do You Know How Your Meal Died?" that appeared in a leading Canadian newspaper (*The Globe and Mail*) on August 26, 2006. At least one researcher has claimed that Wente "recanted" some years after this column appeared—at least to the extent of choosing not to eat meat that had not been certified as free-range—but the present editors have been unable to verify that claim.

ANIMALS

PART

I am not cute, I am not a pet, I am not a mongrel. I am a child, that's all. And I want the walls to become the world all around, like they are for Max. And then he wanted to be where someone loved him best of all and I want that too, that's all I want, really.

S am had just turned nine when those thoughts ran together in his mind; he was young enough not to feel it shameful for the words from a picture book to be going round in his head, and young enough to have his own word for the times that he would be alone and his mind would be running in circles like this: *thinks* was what he called them. Young enough for that, old enough to hardly be able to remember a time when he had lived as a human.

But there had been such a time. For the first five years and more of his life Sam had lived with his mother, Tammy, his brothers, Broderick and Daniel, and his sister, Letitia. He was the youngest and also the weakest, and when the time came that everyone knew he should be talking by, he wasn't, he couldn't. Years later the memory remained fixed in his mind, as strong and as helpless as a headstone, the memory of watching their mouths move, watching their fingers do things in response to the others' moving mouths, and knowing nothing, understanding nothing. He started a habit then of ceaseless babble to compete, to get attention, to make them do things in response to his moving mouth. Perhaps that is always what it is like to be deaf, before you know what deaf is.

It took time for the others to realize he was different. But ever so slowly Broderick and Daniel and Letitia—and after a time even Tammy, their mother—started treating Sam a bit differently. Not that they were less loving, or not exactly that, though in some sense that may have been what it amounted to. They kept saying how cute he was, as one does with a small child, but also as one does with a certain sort of pet, and soon it became clear that the other children loved him in a different way. For the first year or two they had spoken to him as one does to a small person who is constantly changing, constantly able to hear and understand more—and to say more. But as it slowly but steadily became plain that he was not developing in that way, that nothing he said made sense, that he seemed able to understand little or nothing, their way of dealing with him changed too. Slowly but steadily they reverted to baby talk. "Oose a good little Sammy?" they would coo. "Oose a funny wunny little Sammy?" He would look blankly at their moving mouths, or sometimes start making frantic motions with his own mouth.

"There's something wrong with him. You can see it," they would say, "he's not right in the head. If he was, he'd be talking by now—whole sentences, not just words." They were right. He couldn't understand anything of what they were saying. Nor could he hear the traffic, or the rushing of the water in the river, or the thunder in a summer storm. He couldn't hear the phone or the seescreen; he couldn't hear anything.

"Maybe he's a mongrel. They're not just made, you know. A person can give birth to one. And they sometimes look the same as humans, I guess never exactly the same but almost, not so different that you'd know if you weren't trained. Look at his forehead now; a lot of them have that sort of flat little forehead, don't they? And the eyes, so far apart."

Broderick, many years later

I KNOW THE story is just getting started, but I want to interject here just briefly to sketch some of the historical background that the author of the manuscript I've presented you with has not bothered to fill in. This all happened many decades ago, and I'm very aware that for many younger people today the past is largely unfamiliar territory. In those days, if you were a family that discovered it had a mongrel within its midst—that the mother had given birth to a mongrel—you had several choices. First of all, you had the choice of whether or not you would declare it to the authorities; if you did, it would trigger an elaborate bureaucratic process to decide where the creature would be "placed." The decision itself was for the authorities to make, but you would be asked to make a recommendation, and more often than not they would follow that recommendation. You might recommend that the creature remain with the family, but with changed status—as a pet mongrel, in short, not a human child. Alternatively, you could recommend that it be treated as a chattel—which, understandably enough, few families were inclined to do. A surprising number, however, would check "no recommendation," unwilling either to have the status of a former family member changed (so as to reflect the fact that they were keeping a lower order of being) or to put it on a path that would certainly lead to its being lost to them forever. What such families typically did not or would not acknowledge was that, in practice, "no recommendation" generally put the creature on that same path; nine times out of ten a mongrel that started through the bureaucracy with a "no recommendation" from its originating family would end up in the chattel pens.

You might think that some effort would have gone into diagnosis to ensure that those being relabeled *mongrel* or *chattel*, rather than *human*, were being accurately classified. The fact was, though, that diagnosis was an area where thoroughness was noticeably lacking. (To a great extent that remains the case even today.) The doctors were rarely called in to make a judgment as to the precise nature of the defect; the family's word was generally taken at face value, so long as it did not seem to go against the plain facts of the case. Any inspector, even one with minimal medical training, could in almost every case discern those facts pretty quickly. Sometimes it would have that half-vacant look in the eyes that's such a common characteristic of mongrels; in that case it was certainly easy to tell. Various physical abnormalities could also be reliable indicators. Oftentimes too you'd get a distinctive short stature—typically with a somewhat compressed torso, and legs disproportionately long, and a long face, with elongated forehead and jaw—though that was not the only characteristic physical type for mongrels. Sometimes the most salient feature was rounded eyes, unusually far apart and set far forward, making for a disconcertingly inquisitive appearance. Of course lack of verbal ability was very frequently a tip-off. It didn't take a lot of expertise; that was the fact of the matter. Any human could tell a sub-human when he saw one; it was not rocket science.

Not all families in the situation that Tammy Rose and her children found themselves in chose to report their predicament to the authorities. Often enough—perhaps in one of every three cases—the choice would be to keep things quiet. You couldn't pretend to the world that a three-year-old which couldn't talk properly and which didn't look right was human, that much was obvious. But you could simply change your behavior toward it, gradually coming to treat it as a mongrel rather than a fully human being. That way you didn't run the risk of the authorities deciding for whatever reason that no, in this case the family's recommendation wouldn't be followed, this one wouldn't be allowed to stay in the same family, living as a mongrel, this one would be sent to the Repository, or straight to the pens.

Most neighbors in this sort of situation might start to say *Isn't he cute?* in a bit of a different tone, but they would not ask the awkward questions: *What's the matter with your little Jimmy? Why do you call your little one* Bubbles *now?* Or *Percy* or *Freckles* or *Bear?* But never the same name as it had had before—you couldn't have a mongrel with the same name you'd given it when you thought it was human. Or the same food. Any pet had to eat pet food, that was obvious. To be sure, there were families that would feed them scraps from the table. But a line had to be drawn somewhere.

There's a good deal else that could be said but this is enough of a diversion for the time being. I think what I've given you may be enough for now to make the picture a little clearer.

• •

As long as he lived, Sam would always remember the day they took away his knife and fork. Letitia cared about table manners. She fussed about them even more than their mother did; Letty would always be looking at the way he ate. Of course all he had been able to do was watch the others, and he thought things were all right, he thought he was doing pretty well copying them. He didn't notice the way Letitia would glance at him sometimes at mealtimes, despairing, then disparaging, eventually contemptuous—particularly if any of her young friends were over. "He's pathetic, isn't he?" she would say.

Broderick would always cringe when he heard this kind of thing. Like the eldest in so many families, he was both careful and caring. In something of a ponderous way he had developed a real sense of the importance of things. Sometimes it could tilt almost comically into self-importance, but he felt too the importance of things to others. He had heard this sort of nasty silliness about Sam before. Finally it became too much. "It's not the same for him!" he exclaimed angrily one evening as he watched Letty mocking Sam in front of her friends.

Much later in her life Letitia came to realize how she had used that mocking. It wasn't just little Sammy but the whole family, her whole world with its worn floors, its shabby furniture, its hand-me-down clothes, its total lack of the sorts of toys and gadgets that would give a child status in the eyes of her friends. Their mother did her best always, but after their father had left there was never enough money, not really, not so as to keep up any social standing. Back then she never blamed her father; he was never there to blame. Instead it had been her mother, and especially little Sam, who she had blamed, who she had sneered at. If *she* were the one to do it first, if she sneered more loudly and more cruelly at Sam than her friends would ever have dreamed of doing, it would keep their sneers at bay, it would show her to be one of them, a group out of place in this squalor, a group that stood above all this. "It's pathetic!"—that was her favorite phrase. For the tacky lampshades and pictures on the walls, for the rusty car, for the way the spaces under the children's beds had to be used to store tools or sports gear or other odds and ends that were out of season; the tiny house had no attic, no storage room of any kind.

This particular day, the day that Broderick finally snapped at her, she had been pointing at Sam, her mouth wide with glee as the uncomprehending little thing struggled with a plate of spaghetti. Broderick was just coming into the room and must have seen the way Letty had looked at Sam. "It's not the same for him!" he snapped, and instantly was at the table—he had such quick strides for a young boy, Broderick did. He grabbed the knife and fork from Sam's tiny hands. Savagely he sliced into the little pile of spaghetti, cutting it into smaller and smaller pieces. "There," he said, thrusting into Sam's hand the spoon that had been meant for pudding. "See if they feel like laughing at you now!" Letitia still had a twisted little residue of scorn on her face, but fear had pushed it to the margins; Broderick was a husky fourteen and looked a good deal larger than normal when he was fired up like this.

Perhaps you could say that that particular change happened out of good-heartedness. But however you colored them, facts were facts; from that meal onward, Sam never ate with the others or in the same way as the others. Knife and fork were never provided, spoon and bowl became normal routine for him, and it came to be expected that he would eat not at the dining table but in the kitchen, at a little low table in the corner. And mealtime for him would always be a little before or a little after the others had eaten.

One by one the other human things went too. With a lot of gesticulating and wide smiles it was made clear to Sam that the place where he was to sleep would now be a little cot down in the basement. He would have a flannel sheet and heavy blankets, but not the good sheets. They started dressing him in the bright, coarse wool coveralls that you'd see mongrels wearing everywhere. There would be no need for underwear, not anymore, and it would often be a week or ten days before they'd think to put the old coverall in the wash and give him a fresh one. When they did launder his things— his one thing, to be accurate about it—they wouldn't wash what he wore with the others' clothes; it would be a "special load" and their mother would wrinkle up her nose and smile good-humoredly as she held the coverall at arm's length between finger and thumb before dropping it into the machine.

"Boy, does he stink," Daniel or Letitia might say, and sometimes one of them would get the giggles. Sam's body they would wash perhaps once a week. Of course he would break out in little spots and sores now and again, and that too made him less and less human, the change imperceptible on any given day, inescapable week by week, month by month.

The children didn't think much about it either way—even Broderick, who Sam would always believe had loved him. Certainly not Daniel, who had loved Sam since his little brother had been born, in the only way that very young children are able to love a baby sibling—which is to say, in a way virtually indistinguishable from the way in which they love a pet. It can be a strong love, but it can also be a fickle one.

And certainly not Letitia. Much later in life Letty would reach a stage where she loved all the world, but for her such love could never be a place of peace; she was propelled to it out of the tension between the urges that had ruled her as a child and the tenacious conscience that had suddenly taken root in her as she entered adolescence. The tension pumped through Letty's veins a powerful awareness not only of the selfishness and cruelty of the world but also, most painfully, of the selfishness and cruelty that had been a pervasive presence in her own character, aged twelve.

But Tammy cared deeply about Sam. In those years her face could pass for thirty-eight for all the vibrancy and love that could fill it, or for fifty-eight, for all the care and sadness and resentment that filled it too often, too full. Many times she said to Sam with her eyes how sorry she was, how horribly twisted she felt about what was happening to him, what was being done to him. She sometimes thought, too, bleakly and specifically, of what she had done to him. But she was not one to blame herself more than she deserved. For what Sam was going through you could credit equally the quirk of nature that had made the child what he was, the life that Tammy had allowed to go on around him in their own little world, and the life that went on outside, in the wider world—a larger life that pushed the likes of Sam steadily further away from the realm of the human. She could have done more herself, she often thought in later years. Perhaps if Rick had not abandoned them, perhaps if there had been more money. Perhaps if the rest of the world had looked at things differently. But none of that had been the case.

There came a time when things started to go more quickly downhill for Sam. Things were changing day by day for the whole family—especially after the local hospital decided to farm out services to the company putting in the lowest bid, and Tammy lost her job as a cleaner. Tammy had always had the sort of jobs most people wouldn't want to stay at for long, for years stocking shelves in Macy's before they closed down, for years too on the checkout counters at a Your Price store before their scanners were upgraded, then at the hospital. But she had always wanted to stick to it, she was that sort of person. And with each position she had held it had seemed possible that she would be able to do just that. Now it suddenly all looked different. Financial status, social standing—these are words that Tammy didn't much think about. But she knew how much money was coming in, and how much was going out, and she knew she was no longer able to keep up.

Not too long after Tammy had lost the cleaning job she found a new position—lower pay, but a good job, a job with people that valued what she was doing, a job working for the before-and-after-school program in the basement of Sunnyside Primary School. It was a good school, one of the historic old schools in the city core that always seemed to be thriving. But only a few months later that job ended too. The school didn't close, nothing so drastic as that. But enrollment in the before-and-after-school program kept drifting downward, and then the city decided to cut off the base funding they'd been providing for it.

That time Tammy found it hard to figure out just what had gone wrong, just why they'd had to close the program.* The program hadn't been proper day care really, it was just before-and-after-school; maybe it was the wrong sort of program for the neighborhood. One time she and Bonnie—it was Bonnie who really ran the program— had the idea that they would change the routine at the end of the day. They had always said to the parents, "You have to be here to pick up your child by five-thirty at the latest," and just left it at that. The problem had been that a lot of the parents had never paid attention, had arrived at 5:35 or 5:45 or 5:50. Bonnie's idea was that, instead of that, they would now say that for every minute they were late the parents would have to pay extra—$100 for every minute late, no limit. "We'll stay here thirty minutes extra, we won't abandon your little ones. But we're going to be firm about the extra charges." The delinquent parents would feel it—feel it in their wallets; $3,000 for a half hour, that was more than a day's wages for a lot of people.

Tammy and Bonnie couldn't believe what happened. As soon as they had put into place the new policy, the number of people arriving late every day started to go *up*. And it stayed up, settling at a level maybe 20 percent higher than before. That was the attitude people had, people with money, they had a lot of it and they would waste a

---

*[Broderick Clark's note] It certainly wasn't that people were having too few children to keep feeding into the school system—quite the reverse, in fact. But in many areas it seems that they were having fewer *normal* ones. Fewer ones that were human—fully human. And no one had figured out what the problem was. To this day it may be that no one fully understands what happened. Governments had long been offering incentives to encourage childbirth and to help in child raising, had been pouring money into child-care facilities, had been ladling out tax breaks to those who gave birth to more than two children. Understandably enough, it was the middle-class parents who got the tax breaks—and those who were outright wealthy. Many in government and in the media were quite open about the reasons: *We want to give the strongest incentives to the people who can be the best parents, who can raise their children under the most advantageous conditions*, they would say. Much less was offered to those who had less already, who would not be able in any case to offer their children much in the way of the finer things in life.

lot of it sooner than they would trouble themselves to be on time to pick up their children. And perhaps it's not a lot different now.

Perhaps at root what happened to Tammy and her family—to Sam most of all—was a matter of supply and demand. Of being at the right place at the right time too, or not being there—a lot of it was always luck too. You'd think there shouldn't have been any shortage of demand for the services Tammy and Bonnie offered at the before-and-after-school program. Even in an area such as Sunnyside, close to downtown, with a lot of urban professionals, a lot of families were having three kids, or four, where a few generations earlier they might have had only one or two, or none at all. And as much as mongrel births had soared, there were still more than enough human births in a neighborhood like that to keep things growing, that's what you'd think. But more and more of the better-off families were hiring nannies—that was an area where tax breaks were at their most generous. At the other end of the scale, people such as Tammy herself were slipping further and further behind, so that fewer and fewer of them could afford the "luxury" of before-and-after-school care. They had to rely on grandmothers, or friends, or having the older kids take turns looking after the younger ones while the parents worked.

Anyway, there it was, Tammy laid off again. That was in June, at the end of the school year. As demand for child-care workers had shriveled, so too had benefits for those who remained; if you did get laid off, there wasn't a lot you were left with. A bit of severance pay, and that was that. No ongoing healthcare benefits, no pension. For Tammy it was one month's pay for every year worked—little more than six weeks' pay, even if she eked it out carefully. At first the portions of fish and of tofu would get smaller, then there would be no fish or tofu at all most days, only some potatoes or rice and some greens. And then the portions started to get smaller and smaller with each passing day. In those days surely no one was more careful with money than Tammy was—or better at giving to her children a sense that all was well, even as desperation pressed closer and closer.

It was her illness—a case you can still hear people talk of today—that finally brought home to her the urgency of her situation. Brought it home to the children too, all of them. Tammy had never gotten sick, that was one thing she prided herself on. Never. It all turned into something of a cause célèbre. It was a lead item on a lot of newscasts, and it was splashed across the front page of just about every newspaper on the continent. Nobody remembers her name now, of course, but more than a few still remember the story of the woman who ate pet food. Those who do remember the incident at all remember that thousands and thousands of mongrels had become sick, evidently from eating tainted mongrel food. Something in the bonemeal that had been added for protein turned out to be diseased. It was no laughing matter; several hundred pets died. And there was one human hospitalized, a woman at first unidentified who had had to spend several days in the hospital, it was reported, after taking a few bites of pet food herself. As the story went, the woman had taken two or three bites of the stuff as she was trying to entice her pet to try it. "Here, Sammy, try it—you'll see. It's not so bad! Mmm, it really *is* good, you'll see!"

The story sounded more or less plausible, but that wasn't the way it happened at all. To begin with, Sammy was never fed pet food; he might not have been eating at the same table as the others, but Tammy was feeding him the same food, always. Daniel and Letitia and even Broderick might by now have started treating him as only sort of a member of the family, as something no longer entirely loved. And much as she might have hated to face the fact, Tammy was allowing that to happen. But none of them was feeding him pet food. Indeed, there can be little doubt that until Tammy had to be taken to the hospital neither Letitia nor Daniel nor Broderick was for one moment aware that pet food was anywhere to be found in the house. Her whole story, in other words, had been concocted to disguise the fact of her having eaten the food herself—not as a matter of enticing any animal to eat it, but as a matter of what she thought of as staving off severe nutritional deficiency. Like almost everyone back then, and like most people now, Tammy had been given the idea that you need a lot more protein to be healthy than in fact you do. As she saw it, there wasn't near enough to go round. So what she had been doing was giving to her children every last little bit of whatever protein she could afford, which is to say, whatever little bit of goat's milk or tofu she could manage (she could never afford even the poorest grade of ground chattel, of course). And then furtively, after they were all in bed—or, in Sammy's case, curled up on his cot downstairs—she would open a tin of cut-rate pet food, the sort of thing that was mostly filler of some unmentionable sort, ground intestines and strange goo mixed in with vegetable matter and ground-chattel bonemeal.*

If the true story had come out, of course, the whole world would have found out just how hard up Tammy had been, the whole world including all her relatives. And that might have changed things, though it might just as well have made no difference, since the relatives who would certainly have wanted to help were themselves almost as poor as Tammy was, whereas the ones with the means to do so (her uncle Simon, most especially) would just as certainly have found more reason to fault her for her behavior than to come to her assistance. Couldn't she have done better at keeping a job? Why hadn't she had the sense to put something aside for a rainy day?

At any rate, the full story never did come out. Some kind souls felt moved when they heard or read the news reports to send money to help with the hospital bills, so at least her illness had not added any to the family's debts. But there were some debts, and the rent, Tammy had to admit to herself, was now a good deal more than she could afford. They would have to move, she could see that, there could be no doubt about it. Indeed, with her being already three months behind on the rent, the move would have to be soon. And

---

*[Broderick Clark's note] My strong suspicion here is that it would have made no appreciable difference had it instead been "Yum-yums," or another of the premium brands. That was one thing the tainted-pet-food scandal brought out—there often was no difference between buying some of the faniciest brands on the market and buying the lowest, cheapest grade. It turned out that the same company overseas that had been supplying the "no-name" brands had also been selling exactly the same mix to at least three of the best-known and most highly respected North American suppliers—and that the entire batch had been contaminated with melamine, a synthetic compound used as filler in the fertilizer for corn, which in turn was used as gluten filler to eke out the meat. And it turned out to be a lot more toxic than the agricultural scientist had optimistically projected—toxic enough to kill small animals and to make larger ones extremely ill.

it would have to be done on the quiet, so they'd be well out of town before the landlord had any idea they were gone.

The one place where demand for child-care workers was holding up well, even increasing, was in the border towns. The border seemed to mean less and less with each passing month but there still *was* a border; the patrols and the border guards with their trained wolverines, the barbed wire, and the alarms were all still in place. Every day dozens died trying to get across and dozens more were captured—but hundreds and hundreds succeeded. It was these people even more than the established citizens who were having children, not three or four, but five or six, even eight or ten children. And as the border towns swelled and the illegals found work (there was *always* work for illegals) they all needed child care. Inexpensive child care. Most of it was informal, of course; the pay was absurdly low, and there were no benefits at all, but it *was* work, and work that Tammy knew how to do.

Would that be enough? Every night, in the middle of the night, for weeks, as she awaited the end of the month—they would wait until the night before rent was again due before they made their move— Tammy would lie awake wondering whether it would be enough. Going over and over again the sums for food, for rent, for the few little things that one had to have above and beyond food and rent, even if one was poor. Not the dance lessons that Letty had had that one year, that one good year three years back, not those certainly; not the new mitt Broderick so wanted for his baseball, just pickup baseball, no fancy team with their fancy uniforms and their travel and their fees, just the sandlot, that was all, but no, he couldn't have that glove either, and no clarinet for Daniel—no, any of those things were out of the question.

And for Sammy? That was when Tammy's head began to pound, for she knew there was one thing she could do, something that would make it so much easier for the other three children. And would it make it worse for Sammy? Her heart stabbed with the knowledge of how little she could give him, how much he needed, how everything was changing, not just for the five of them but with the world. She ached with her desire—no, with her need—to make it all better for him. But with every day, and especially at night, at two in the morning, at three in the morning, she was weighed down more and more with the certainty of how little she could do for him. He would be better somewhere else, with someone else, with people who could . . . Well, it would just be better, if she could find the right household. Then, even as a mongrel, he would be taken care of better than she could afford for any of her children.

The next day—it was a bright morning in late June—their landlord, Mr. Conrad, came round to see them. He had been coming most every week the past while, and every time it was the same. He shifted his weight from foot to foot and looked down at a grimy crack between the floorboards as he scratched on about how the rent hadn't been there, it hadn't been there on the first of the month again, and that was weeks ago now, it hadn't been there any of the other times she had promised it since. It had to be there on the first of the month, everyone knew there had to be rules, he just couldn't keep allowing some people to be late. This wasn't the first time, he thought they should know that perfectly well.

He would never shout or even get sharp when he would go on like this. But he always made sure he came round when Broderick and Daniel and Letitia and Sam were all there—that increased the shame of it, there were books that said how much more likely a tenant was to pay up if she were shamed in front of her family, her children especially, the statistics were remarkable, really. Usually Tammy would glare and huff and press forward until the confrontation was happening out in the hall where it could only be half heard. But this time she just stayed silent, the muscles stretched taut in her face, and she waited until he was done. She told him as she always did that he would have his money soon, very soon. But then when he was gone she pressed her face into her hands and rocked back and forth slowly, staring at the handle of the door that Mr. Conrad had just closed. Sam could see her mouth and it was open as if to cry out, but he did not think she was making any sound. It might have been for two or three minutes she stood like that, and then she turned almost savagely away from the door and in a few minutes was directing the children—all of them, Sammy too—very calmly, as if from a great distance. They packed everything into a few old boxes. She had "pulled herself together," as the saying goes, and they were moving.

It was still dark when she came to Sammy, curled asleep on his little cot, in his blankets. She had scissors with her, and a needle and thread, and quietly she took up his coverall and found a place where the fabric was doubled, and made a slit and slipped into it a folded paper, wrapped in plastic so it would be protected. Sitting quietly as the half light began to seep through the high basement window, she sewed the letter—for that was what it was, a letter— into the coverall.

My Sam,

I am leaving this with you, hoping that some day you will somehow be able to understand it, and understand what I am doing now. We will be off in the morning for Brownsburg, me and Letty and Broderick and Daniel. I have thought and thought and now I know I cannot be bringing you with us. I will be leaving you with the Stinsons, they are good people I think, with all my heart I shall pray you come to no harm. I think what I am doing is for the best, the best for you as well as the rest of us, but I am not knowing this. Sometimes I am thinking there is nothing we can know, really. My heart is breaking with love for you and for the terrible hole I have dug for us all. But I cannot provide for you four, all of you, not now, I cannot take care of you, not properly. I will think of you always and always ache for you, and always be hoping that you are well, that what I am doing now will have made it better for you, for I know there is a chance it could be worse, even much worse. I know that sometimes in lives there is no end, and all we can do is try to hold something good in our hearts and remember that we were once loved, that someone somewhere loves us still. I hope someday you can read this or have it read to you. But not soon, not so soon—I would love so much for you to have the words and be hearing, be reading, but not reading this when the hurt is still strong and soon.

Then she had written "love," of course, and signed it "your Mother, always." There was another line too, a line that she had scratched out or tried to scratch out, it was crossed over again and again but if you held it up to a window you could still read where it said "when you were born you were the light of my life."

Sam was stirring as she finished sewing the little package into the seam of the coverall. He looked up at her; there was red around her eyes and she had red blotches on her cheek and neck, and tears streaming down. She bundled him in all his blankets and took him in her arms, knowing it would be the last time. He was much too old and too heavy to be carried like this. Her tears fell on his forearms, and on his small face. She staggered a little going down the porch steps, and again just over halfway down the block, but she made it to the Stinsons' front yard, up the little rise around the corner on 10th Street.

That was where the neighborhood started to change. The Stinsons had made a lot of money on that very change, as a matter of fact, buying up properties when prices were still low, and then turning a tidy profit unloading them as gentrification had spread to 12th, 11th, and now to 10th Street as well. They had fixed up 102 themselves—at any rate that was a phrase Carrie Stinson would often use, "we did it up ourselves," she would tell people seeing the inside of the house for the first time, looking at the skylights, the Italian tile, the new kitchen, the loft attic, but of course they hadn't done all that with their own hands, they had had people in for the actual building, it was the arranging of it, the choosing, that had been entirely handled by the Stinsons themselves.

They had just one child and no pets—in fact there were no mongrels at all along the entire block. They had always smiled at Tammy, at all the children, Sam included, and once when Tammy was struggling with bags and packages and a stroller when Letitia and Sam were still very small, the Stinsons had helped her pick up a number of items that had fallen out of her bag and gone skittering into the gutter. Mr. Stinson—he had an odd first name, "Zayne," it was—had looked awkward as he had tried to find places to put the things he had retrieved from the sidewalk, and had ended up piling them a bit askew on top of the awning of the stroller. Awkward, and a bit comical. But very friendly, and both of them had seemed to speak kindly; Tammy had remembered that.

There was starting to be more light in the sky but there was still a chill in the air as she set Sam down ever so gently on the Stinsons' porch, still wrapped in his blankets, and held him for a moment even closer than she had when she had been carrying him. With a half-strangled sound and an awkward gesture she somehow made it plain to him that he was to stay there, that he was not to follow her, but that she loved him, he could see that she loved him, *please see that I love you* came silently from her lips, and the tears did not stop as she turned and fumbled with the gate by the sidewalk, and walked quickly but not steadily back toward the house that she was about to leave with her other children, back to the boxes that had to be piled in the car before full light, she would have to try to have them out of there with everything they were able to pack into the rusty old Honda by full light, it wouldn't do to have the neighbors see her leaving like that as they came out in the morning, certainly not that nasty Thelma two doors down, who knew Mr. Conrad, who could so easily call him and have him come round again, and then the police would come—no, they must be out of there, out of there right away.

PART

2

Broderick, many years later

AT THIS POINT I think it makes sense to offer a few comments and to try to answer a few questions that I imagine may have been occurring to some of you. People used to say that it would be absurd to imagine a deaf person being mistaken for a mongrel. But I'd hazard it's no more surprising than a white person being mistaken for a black person if they have a dark complexion, or if they blacked up their skin. And that has certainly happened often enough—people not looking beyond one salient feature. That just seems to be the way humans work. So what can I say about deaf people and mongrels? The fact is it *did* happen. It happens still, and not all that infrequently, either. Maybe a lot of times it's partly chance—a child being born not only deaf but with a strangely shaped forehead, and with some of the elongation in parts of the face that you often see in a more pronounced way among mongrels. And then, of course, there's the fact that even then *mongrel* was becoming such a broad category; no matter what people say, it wasn't as straightforward as it once might have been to pick out a mongrel on appearance alone.

But there's probably more to it than that, most times. If you notice, it seems never to happen that a deaf child in a well-off family ends up being mistaken for a mongrel. But in a poor family—and you have to remember the poor mostly just don't go to doctors, haven't done so for generations now—the mother and her child exist pretty much out of sight of the medical system. And, of course, what had for a time long ago seemed a great dawn of promise for the deaf, the age of cochlear implants, had collapsed in the wake of the studies linking those devices to a wide variety of neurological disorders, as well as to a greatly increased likelihood of brain tumors. It was perhaps no wonder that in an age of scarce resources a good deal less attention began to be paid to diagnosing anything for which there was no easy cure. And that was particularly the case—if I may be allowed to restate the obvious—for those who would have no means of paying for any effective treatment, let alone a cure, even if effective treatment or anything close to a cure had been available to them. Deafness became an abnormality that placed a child in something of a twilight zone, and there may in fact have been some unacknowledged societal logic to the way in which those afflicted could become categorized as mongrels.

Of course no mother will imagine at first that there could be any abnormality that isn't glaringly obvious. But if a child turns out to be a slow developer, doesn't talk until he's one and a half, or two, or two and half even, and then only minimally, if it gets to that point where it becomes clear something is wrong with it, you can understand the mother's first fear will be that she gave birth to a mongrel. In the era we're talking about, she would have known—anybody knew—that mongrel births were becoming more common. She would not be able to stop herself from thinking of the horror of that, and oftentimes she would not know the other possibilities. If that happened it wouldn't take much to lead her to act as Tammy acted. And others too would have assumed just what she assumed about a child that could speak not at all or only in a lisping and primitive way. Even then, everyone had been habituated over many years to think in terms of the dichotomy, mongrels and chattels or humans, humans or mongrels and chattels. And the Repositories, starved of funds as they had been, the staffs overworked, worn down—how often did they have the inclination, let alone the resources, to send a creature for all the tests? Easier to make the assumption that would be right nine times out of ten, ninety-nine times out of a hundred, and get on with it. That's just how things happened, there's no more to it than that. Human error, people slipping through the cracks—when has it not gone on?

That said, it was only as economic conditions changed, and particularly after the great extinctions occurred, that things started to become much chancier for those that had been born deaf.* No one quite said as much,

---

*[Here and elsewhere where footnotes to Broderick Clark's material appear in these pages, they have, unless otherwise indicated, been supplied by Clark.] In the early twenty-first century, in the twentieth century even, doctors had been better trained to pick up on deafness. A wide range of treatments was available, sign language and lipreading were commonly practiced, and the typical deaf person lived a life very largely integrated into human society.

but the fact was that with what were reported to be significant nutritional shortages and with medical resources so scarce, it seemed to be to everyone's advantage to keep to a minimum the number of humans suffering from conditions that were expensive to treat. Deformed creatures who not long before would have led a prolonged if hardly pleasant existence at vast public expense were now allowed to expire quietly early in life. And many who would in an earlier age have been classified as suffering from one or another of a long list of abnormalities were more and more frequently lumped in with the class of mongrels and chattels. (It had long been acknowledged that the twentieth- and early twenty-first-century practice of treating several varieties of mongrel as fully fledged humans was as ruinously expensive as it was psychologically painful.)

But let me go back a step, and run over what actually happened so far as mongrels are concerned. I am sure it's familiar ground for some of you, but others may not know the history. The word *mongrel* as it is used today is itself something of an etymological mongrel. It partakes in the primary meaning we give to it nowadays both of its own centuries-old etymological history and of that of the word *mongo*, coincidentally related to it both in sound and in denotation. Not all that long ago—as recently as the first half of the twenty-first century—*mongrel* was primarily used to refer to a dog or other domestic animal that was not a purebred, though it could also be used as an adjective to refer to almost any strange or unlikely genetic mixture. Not in those days, but not all that long before, no more than a few decades earlier, *mongo* (or the variant *mongoid*) was a very precise term for a certain sort of defective, a subclass of what we would now call a mongrel. That coinage originated when James Langford Peake published his "Inquiry Into the Ethnic Element of Idiocy" in 1870; he quite rightly observed the degree to which the creatures he was describing, though born to Caucasian parents, resembled the peoples of the Mongo River region of North Africa. *Mongan idiocy* was the name he gave it. The category of *mongrel* is nowadays much broader, of course, embracing literally dozens of the old "micro" categories of defective; from one angle it is simply a red herring nowadays to make any direct association of *mongrel* with *mongo* or *mongoid*. But there is a historical connection, and I am among those who find the result telling if one tries to trace that. Surprisingly few people these days are aware of how the narrow old categories came to be replaced by the broader and more comprehensive ones that reflect our modern understanding of proper taxonomy.

The base from which that understanding grew was the class known as *mongos*, or *mongans* (occasionally *mongoids*). When Peake identified these creatures he saw them as a subspecies; they were understood not to be human, or at least not to be human in the same way and to the same extent as you and I. Not only did they look different; they typically had far lower levels of intelligence. If they could speak at all it tended to be largely gibberish. They were susceptible to a wide range of medical problems that led naturally in most cases to an early death. And nature was allowed to take its course—that is a key point. Mongans in the nineteenth century were not subjected to unnatural cruelty, to systematic mistreatment and crammed into factory farms as they are now. But nor were they given a lot of special treatment to try to make them live artificially long lives.

That all changed radically over the course of the twentieth century. Ironically enough, this was an age in which Western civilization purported to value what was natural. But that was just how people liked to think of themselves; the reality was very different. People would apply cosmetics and undergo surgery to make themselves look more natural; they would rearrange the landscape to give it a more natural look. The rhetoric of the natural pervaded discussions of food too—and, for that matter, discussions of topics such as human disability. But here again rhetoric belied reality; with farm animals and with the groups that we now class together as mongrels, twentieth- and early twenty-first-century Western civilization went to unnatural extremes, in entirely opposite directions.

In one direction people began to act as if the various groups we now class as mongrels were not sub-human at all—in the case of the most prominent subset of defectives, the mongoids, the very word was effectively banned. (For several generations people referred to mongoids as "people with Peake's syndrome.") Vast amounts of money were spent on researching their condition and on trying to lengthen and improve their lives. They were given schooling—and not only that, they were schooled in the same classrooms as humans with normal intelligence. People spoke always of mongans and other forms of mongrel being "slower" than others, of their being subject to language and cognitive "delay," of how they could "continue to increase language acquisition skills into adulthood." Rarely was it admitted that, however much they might slowly improve, the cognitive and language skills of many mongrels would never reach the level of the average preschooler, let alone the average adult. The fact was, no matter how much training a mongrel received, it would almost always never be able to enunciate properly, never be able to *think* properly, not even when using simple words. At best, mongrels would use the simple present tense, with a tiny vocabulary, and with habits of pronunciation that made it all but impossible for anyone who didn't spend a good deal of time among them to understand anything of what they were saying. Their severe handicaps tended to be glossed over by the social services doublespeak of the era ("They make good use of the speech and language skills they have, over the same range of communicative activities as everyone else, particularly if encouraged to do so by sensitive support"). All well and good so long as one accepts the normal human "range of communicative activities" as coming to a stop a long way short of what you or I are capable of.

Of course the scientists and social scientists did learn a few things with all that effort and all that research. Even when you had made allowances for exaggeration and euphemism you still had to admit that the average mongrel had developed, with all this human help, the ability to communicate a good deal more effectively than a dog or a dolphin, even than a chimpanzee. And had developed a few practical abilities too. Not just how to pack groceries (though it was proven that a mongrel could sometimes manage a job of that sort in the real world), but things such as sign language as well; some authorities, indeed, claimed mongrels were better able to learn a language that bypassed the ears and mouth. The research led to real discoveries too. Perhaps most important in the specific case of mongans, researchers learned the biological basis for the disease—members of that group had an odd number of chromosomes (in the opposite direction of what one might have expected; rather than having anything missing, it was an extra chromosome that threw them off). But the researchers, and the people who funded the research, treated that discovery as no more than part of the background to their ongoing effort to diagnose and treat mongans. They failed to see it in its true light, as confirmation of the simple fact that mongans—and mongrels generally, had they been classifying things at that time in the broader fashion we have come to understand as more appropriate—were simply not fully human.

(I don't imagine many today would think, "How can something not fully human emerge from a human womb?" We're not used to thinking that way now. I can tell you there was a time, though, when such questions were put frequently, and with feeling. That was in the days before the reproductive revolution, of course—mongrels were not yet being cloned—so it wasn't, as it is now, only a small percentage of mongrels that came from a human womb. It was all of them. Every single mongrel that lived emerged from a human womb, and to some people—a minority of cranks and crackpots they may have been, but they were a loud minority—that was all that needed to be known. Case closed: they were us, essentially. All it took to demolish those sorts of arguments was one simple fact. A mule comes out of the womb of a horse, and it is not a horse. More than that: at some point in evolutionary history the first member of what we now call the human species came out of the womb of a creature that we would now classify as a member of another species. This reality is obvious to almost everyone nowadays.)

In the mid-twenty-first century, of course, the pendulum started to swing back toward where it had been in the nineteenth century—at least when it came to the treatment of mongrels. (There was never any question of returning directly for that one variety of mongrel to the term *mongo* or *mongan*, though.) Partly the swing back can be attributed to what one might call *necessary* neglect. What was true for deaf people was doubly the case for mongrels: how could you justify putting the resources—the time as well as the money—into improving their lot when so many of the fully human were in such desperate straits? And so, slowly but surely, mongrels lost that "sensitive support" that had nurtured the development of their mental abilities in general and their verbal skills in particular. The mental condition of the average mongrel deteriorated, and so too did its physical condition. It was not only that no new treatments were being developed; it was also that the old treatments were falling into disuse. The special drugs, the funding for extra educational help, the special facilities for mongrels who could not be cared for by relatives—it all drained away. A mongrel's average lifespan began to spiral lower and lower, back toward exactly where it had been in the late nineteenth and early twentieth centuries, in fact. And, just as surely, if perhaps more imperceptibly, the status of a mongrel shifted; without always being able to articulate the feeling, humans for the most part no longer looked at mongrels in quite the same way.

I should make clear that some of the terminology here is almost bound to be anachronistic in one direction or another; there was so much change going on—changes in classification systems and linguistic changes as much as changes in societal attitudes and changes in circumstance for the mongrels themselves. Certainly it wasn't at all a simple matter of those who had been classified in different ages as *mongans* or as *sufferers from Peake's syndrome* being slowly reclassified. A wide range of congenital conditions, syndromes, and disorders were in similar, overlapping situations. Those with physical deformities as well as those with cognitive ones came to be seen as part of the picture. (And not unreasonably so, at least from a societal point of view; one affected by what was once discussed only under the narrow sub-category of Sellars' dystrophy is no more capable of becoming a full member of society than is one affected by what was once discussed only under the narrow sub-category of Peake's syndrome. I have said that deafness may occupy something of a shadowy middle ground, but it is certainly arguable that a creature born deaf, dumb, and blind may be fairly placed in the same category as one with cognitive defects arising from other conditions—and that is, of course, how extremes of that sort have eventually come to be viewed.) And as the status of those affected drifted downward and scarce resources began again to be directed more toward helping the fully human, lines of a significant debate over taxonomy began to be drawn within scientific and medical circles. For centuries the trend had been toward ever narrower categories, in this area of taxonomy as in so many others. But did the struggle to be ever more precise, to categorize things in an ever narrower and narrower fashion always serve a useful purpose? And how much of the truth did the conclusions capture? You could make a plausible case on either side of an issue like that, but over time a consensus emerged: the sort of classification system which made the greatest sense in the real world in a case such as this was the one that harmonized best both with underlying categories and with the realities of what would constitute appropriate and acceptable treatment for these various related types, in a world made up of humans. If the reality for those affected by Gyberger's syndrome and Peake's syndrome and Wilson's disorder and dozens of others was broadly similar, then for functional purposes these could reasonably be regarded not as three or four or twenty or thirty categories, but as one. With sub-categories within it, of course—but in the essentials, one broad category. Once that sort of reordering was achieved, there could be no significant barrier to the broadening of the category of *mongrel* so that it could serve in its present capacity, encompassing dozens of sub-categories once regarded as subject to meaningful distinctions. As more and more people realized, there was little point in splitting hairs.

The downgrading of those who were coming to be lumped together as mongrels was well underway even before the great extinctions. In the wake of the extinctions, and especially with the development of the whole industry of chattel farming, the trend quite naturally intensified; no conceivable purpose could be served by a chattel developing any mental skills above and beyond the ability to understand and follow very simple commands.

No doubt the "enlightened" populace of, say, a century ago would be appalled were they to see the practices of today when it comes to the treatment of mongrels and chattels.* They might do well to remember how

---

*For those with a historical bent, the etymology of the word *chattels* may be of interest. Long ago people used the word *chattels* simply to mean "belongings," but included within this use people who belonged to other people. I don't mean voluntarily, the way a person will say to another, "I belong to you"; I mean people "belonging" to other people even against their will. To be a chattel in that sense was not a pretty thing, not at all. In England until well into the nineteenth century a wife was legally considered a chattel of her husband, with no rights over money or property she had earned or had been given, no rights even over her own children. Even worse was *chattel slavery*: that was the term used to denote systems of slavery under which slaves were considered to exist only as their owners' property, a condition that would be passed on from generation to generation. All that eventually changed, of course, at least under the law, and for almost two centuries no one used the word *chattel* in anything other than a historical sense. When the word began to enter the language again with this new meaning signifying a functional distinction between mongrels adopted as pets and mongrels who would be used for labor and for consumption, there was some initial discomfort about the reintroduction of the term, particularly among those who were sensitive to the ways in which it had been associated with both slavery and the oppression of women. Really it was not until just the past few years, with the changes wrought by the reproductive revolution, that such discomfort has eased to the extent that now the extremist vegetarians are almost the only ones to express any criticism of

economics and expediency shaped their own practices with regard to their fellow creatures. To remember how, over the course of a little more than half a century, they had quietly changed virtually every aspect of the lives of the creatures whose milk they drank and whose flesh they ate. People for the most part forget history; I hope that those who remember it will forgive me these sometimes lengthy interpolations, for I do think it important for people now to see against a larger canvas what has happened. In America in the early 1950s cattle grazed in open fields for almost all their lives, pigs were allowed space to poke about and wallow, chickens could leave the coop to peck about. By the dawn of the twenty-first century the lives of all those creatures had been made uniformly wretched. Beef cattle spent much of their lives tramping through their own feces in overcrowded feedlots, eating food that was not easy for them to digest but that would make their flesh more fully marbled with fat when humans ate that flesh; pigs were confined for their entire lives in tiny steel and concrete pens; and dairy cattle, bred so that their massive udders inhibited almost any movement, never left the factory milking complex. The lives of laying hens were the worst of all. Crammed together in wire cages stacked several rows high, with each tiny cage holding several chickens and with the droppings from the upper cages falling on those below, they lived their entire lives with the ammonia smell of their feces, overpowering, unrelenting. It was considered normal for the creatures leading such an existence to become desperate and vicious; each one would have its beak trimmed so it could not gouge and destroy the others in its tiny cage.

America was by some distance the worst. (Or, to put it another way, America was *the consistent leader in achieving new levels of efficiency and profitability in intensive farming*.) But in every Western country and in

---

the continuing use of the term. More and more, chattels are becoming creatures that no one could confuse with humans, creatures clearly of a categorically lower order. But to me at least, the term remains objectionable—and we should continue to object to it, just as we should continue to object to the cruel excesses of intensive farming. Fundamentally, a chattel remains no different from a mongrel, and to my mind, that is what we should call it; we should face squarely and be prepared to justify through honest argument our willingness to eat the flesh of mongrels, just as in an earlier age people had an obligation to face squarely and be prepared to justify their willingness to eat the flesh of a cow, a chicken, a horse, a lamb—or, in many cultures, a dog.

many others, animals came more and more to be subjected to conditions that amounted to ceaseless torture. And for what? Not simply in order to be eaten: for thousands of years humans had made a practice of eating their fellow creatures without feeling any need to subject those creatures to appalling conditions for their entire lives. No, what happened in the second half of the twentieth century happened simply in order to make what was produced from their flesh and milk available ever more cheaply to the consumer, ever more profitably for the producer. And this slide into production methods that amounted to endlessly efficient torture took place in an era when the economy was steadily growing. People in those days had not the excuse of a twenty-year depression and an environmental upheaval such as the one that was caused by the great extinction of species.

So why did they do it—and how was it possible to do it without arousing mass protests? Why were so few consciences troubled? Well, some of us have our theories.* Certainly it was not often necessary to answer pleas

---

*As to the underlying causes, it may have been a time of great wealth, but that was surely not the case for everyone. The rich and the very rich became richer still during those years. But the average person's wages never quite kept up with rising costs, and the number who truly struggled kept rising. At a conscious level the better-off told themselves that the whole process was just a sifting according to what everyone deserved; if the poor found it harder and harder to get by, they had only themselves to blame for what they had done, or, more likely, what they had failed to do. But at another level something nagged away, saying that however the poor had gotten to be where they were, they needed to be kept from turning against the established order—against freedom, against the system that had given them the opportunity to improve themselves (even though they manifestly had failed to take up that opportunity).

What would it take to keep them contented? Contented enough, at least, not to cause any trouble? The seescreen's predecessors—television and the Internet— made a big difference, of course, and most things electronic kept getting less and less expensive the whole time. But also alcohol, and fat. A quart of vodka cost five dollars in America in 1950. And a pound of hamburger cost fifty cents. Fifty-five years later, real disposable income had gone up very considerably. It had gone up for those at the top, but for those in the middle too, and even for some near the bottom of the heap. Costs for most things had gone up too, of course, though not as much as wages; in terms of most people's purchasing power most things had become a bit less expensive. But meat and alcohol had led the way, by a big margin.

That had not always been the pattern. Between 1900 and 1950 meat became relatively more expensive; the prices of flour and sugar went up by about four times, while the price of hamburger went up by about six times. Between 1950 and 2000,

for animals to be treated better; that's one important thing. The truth of what went on in the intensive farms of the late twentieth and early twenty-first centuries may have been an open secret, but it *was* largely kept secret. The feedlots for beef cattle, the pig barns, the vast chicken sheds—and, of course, the slaughterhouses and the rendering plants—were kept well away from the eyes of the public. If any reporter wanted to discover and to tell the truth about what went on behind those fences and walls, it was extraordinarily difficult for her or for him to do so. But of course not many reporters did want to tell those particular truths, and not many newspapers or television stations wanted to print or broadcast them, and not many people wanted to read about them or see them, which was why not many newspaper or television stations wanted to . . . And so it went.

In the early twenty-first century, though, quite a few people began to take a rather different approach, began to quite brazenly admit what was going on and embrace it with a willful disregard of conscience. In many

---

the half century in which factory farming took over, that pattern was reversed. The price of sugar went up sevenfold, and prices on average went up by eight or nine times, while average wages went up by about twelve times. But the price of hamburger went up by only six times. In terms of how it related to purchasing power, then, hamburger was for the average wage earner half as expensive at the end of those fifty years as it had been at the beginning. Factory-farmed eggs, the product for which the agricultural industry achieved perhaps the greatest number of "efficiencies," went up in price by no more than a factor of four over the second half of the twentieth century. The only comestible to rival factory-farmed eggs in real price decline over those same fifty years was hard liquor, which went up by between three and four times. And to repeat, over the same period wages went up by a factor of twelve; you can do the math from there. Even if your income rose more slowly than did average prices—as happened for most people in America, for example, in decades such as the 1980s and 2000s—liquor and fatty foods kept getting cheaper and cheaper to buy.

For the most part, though, the steady decline in the real prices of the ultimate comfort foods, fatty meat and booze, was a fact never acknowledged. Even as America became, of all nations in human history, the one spending the lowest percentage of its gross domestic product on food, it remained for most an article of faith that food was expensive. You could in those years generally counter any plea for farm animals to be treated more humanely simply by reference to cost: supporters of free-range meat, eggs, and dairy products were charged with being elitists all too willing and ready to take food out of the mouths of the less fortunate, who supposedly could not afford the 20, 30, or 50 percent mark-up on nourishment more humanely produced.

circles it became entirely acceptable to confess to one's friends that, much as one might not want to keep hearing about such things, one was aware of what was going on. And not just to one's friends: I once found in some old clippings my great-grandfather had kept a newspaper piece, from 2004 or 2005 it might have been, in which one of the columnists—an unusual name, Want, or Went, the heading had been half eaten away so I couldn't easily make it out—was quite blunt about it:

> [L]ots of chefs have already kicked *foie gras* off the menu. They think it isn't nice to torture animals before you eat them. Indeed, most of what we do to animals before we eat them isn't nice. If we knew exactly how they lived and died, we'd be horrified. Fortunately for us, we're so removed from where our food comes that we can choose not to know. Ignorance is bliss, and I, for one, am a devoted carnivore. I have studiously tried to avoid learning about the revolting details of factory farming, because if I knew, then I would have to stop eating meat and start sending money to the animal-rights movement, or at the very least search out meat that had an okay life. That would be hard. It's easier to be a hypocrite.

That much, at any rate, is very largely the same—has become very largely the same as it was long ago, with the development once more of intensive farming. Once again many people are quite willing to admit openly that they more or less know that what they are doing is hideously wrong. They just don't want to *really* know.

But I am getting ahead of myself; you must forgive me. I get altogether too involved when it comes to some of these issues, when it comes to a great deal of this. It's in part for that reason that I am not trying to tell you the story myself, merely interjecting comments from time to time. But that is far from the only reason. As I hope I made clear in my introductory remarks, this is not a story I know in as much detail as I would like. And certainly I know little of it "from the inside," much as I have long been familiar with its broad outlines. It is for me, after all, in a very real sense, a story of family, however long lost. Still, I am not anything even faintly resembling a born storyteller. Quite the opposite, indeed: I am unashamedly a man of fact rather than of imagination. But I am aware that imagination matters—that it may matter a very great deal. For all these reasons I think it better to let the story come to you through the manuscript that I have placed before you all. I feel sufficiently strongly on that score that even where the author is presenting my own "character" I have let stand what has been written, without protest and without revision. It does not always map precisely onto my own recollections of what happened or of how things felt—but then again, how confident can we ever be of the degree to which our own memories retain the true feel of the past, even of our own past? It was all so very long ago.

One other related comment. I am not for the moment revealing the authorship of this narrative, or how a copy of the manuscript came into my possession. I suspect that were you to be aware now of who has written what is before you, you would continually be distracted by present-day, real-world questions—*What sort of person is the author now? How does this or that character compare to the one of long ago?* and so on. Reasonable questions, no doubt, but I think they get in the way of parts of the story that matter more—and that deserve to be more fully colored by imagination.

• •

Naomi always woke up early. On a school day she would lie in bed and plan the hours ahead, thinking everything through to the tiniest detail. Today, like every day almost, her mother would make her porridge for breakfast, it would be the proper oatmeal, please make it the proper oatmeal, not the awful cream of wheat. This was Tuesday, Tuesday was always quiz day for math, she could make up practice questions for herself, that would be good. Social studies would be Australia again and that was good too, maybe it would still be Australia all week. She liked all that about the rocks and the desert and the koalas and even all the deadly snakes. And after school Winifred and Katie and everyone were going to meet up with her at the old fairgrounds by the river and they would make their way to their hideout, the tree fort was what they called it, but that maybe made it sound grander than it was. Still, it had taken a lot of boards to build, and it didn't really matter if it looked just right, it was sturdy enough and large enough to hold all three of them, even one or two more, and they had hauled all the wood there themselves and nailed each piece until it was really stuck. And then nailed a little bit more to be extra sure, some of the nails had been bent over when they were hammered and you couldn't count those ones, not really.

They always told their parents when they were going to the tree fort that they were going to the park, and it wasn't a lie—the fort was hidden deep in the woods at the park's far end, right near where the old abandoned factories backed onto the park. Probably people had wanted to keep the dense woods there so no one could see through to all the rubble and empty concrete; whatever, it made it the perfect hideaway, they could spend hours there and maybe they would today but sometimes you could get hungry if you were there for hours, maybe tonight she would help Daddy make the spaghetti and cheese casserole, the one she loved so much, the one you had to bake in the oven to cook it again once you had cooked it the first time on top of the stove, they hadn't had that in weeks and weeks now.

Naomi's plans came to a stop. There was a sort of whinnying noise from outside her window—no, perhaps it was a bit to the left, and down. Right near the corner of the veranda, that would make it, they had a big veranda, everyone always made a fuss talking about that when they saw the place for the first time. Naomi slept in the front of the house, and Mommy and Daddy slept in the big bedroom in the back, sort of they did but mainly in the night Daddy would go downstairs and sleep on the little bed in the study. It still left another big bedroom and another little bedroom as spares, but Mommy always said she was going to make the one on the south side her studio when she took up painting again. Except for Naomi no one had a view of the front. She got up now, pulling her blankie around her, she was too old to have a blankie now, years too old her parents told her, especially her mother told her but sometimes when it was still half dark and there were noises a person might want a blankie. She could hear the noises better when she came to the window, they were like tears, that sort of noise. And they were coming from the veranda, yes, she could hear it clearly, it was just like crying. She held her blankie tight around her as she crept down the stairs, maybe she should wake her parents but it was such a little sound, the sort of little sound that came from a little creature, and she was a little creature herself, Daddy would always call her his little one, somehow it seemed right that she should be the one to be exploring when it sounded like another little one.

You had to put both hands on the lock to turn it if you were little, and then the bolt would click and it would move, it all fit right inside the door when it wasn't doing its lock work. She peered outside. Way over by the wicker furniture at the far end of the veranda was what looked like a small shape. It was wrapped in a blankie too, no, in real blankets, thick ones, several of them all thick and warm. But it was shivering. Naomi went a little closer and she could see that the noise that had sounded like tears really was tears, they ran down the little face that poked out above the blankets. And then it started to go quiet, the noise almost stopped, but Naomi knew you could be just as cryey, just as much feeling hurt inside, when you were very quiet, sometimes she cried like that under the covers when she knew she wasn't supposed to be making a noise, wasn't supposed to be awake, wasn't supposed to be sad.

She started ever so slowly, ever so quietly to move toward it. As soon as its lips moved she knew it was a mongrel. She heard the gurgle where proper words should be. And she knew she wanted to keep it, wanted to hold it and make it warm, wanted to make it her special friend. Her mother and father had told her she couldn't have a mongrel, mongrels were too much trouble, she'd lose interest in it, in the end half of them had to be sent to the Repositories anyway, in the end people who kept mongrels got tired of them, that was just a fact, half the time or even more than half the time it didn't work out. But Naomi knew it wouldn't be like that with her, not with a little one that was hers—one like this one that was a little creature and also a good creature. Her mother and father had told her she could sometimes know inside herself if someone else had a good heart or a not-so-good one, and it was true, she could, she knew Mr. Carruthers at the corner store was a bad person no matter what anyone said, he did things with his hands behind the counter that made you want to run away before you had paid for your candy, and Ms. Riis at the library, *rhymes with* fleece, she would always say, *not* rice, *not* nice, but she was nice, she was good, you could know that.

"Where's your home, little one? Did you lose your way? Maybe your keeper's worried about you." She reached out to pat the creature on the head, to stroke its shoulders and its back, and it shivered a little closer to her. A snivel came into the crying, and the creature gurgled. "There, there, you'll be safe now, I'll take care of you." Her mother and her father would have to let her keep it, they would just have to.

"We can't keep it, Gnome, you know that." It was Daddy's voice. Naomi was too old now for pet names but she hadn't told them yet, sometimes it was hard to tell things to your mom and mad. She thought of that before she thought of the meaning of what her father had said. He had come up behind her so quietly that Naomi had not heard him. "You know what your mother has said about having another creature around the house. And I've said it too," he added, remembering somewhat belatedly the importance of parental solidarity. "This one's been abandoned, you can tell it's not lost or it wouldn't have the blankets wrapped around it. It would just be wandering around and sniffing about, maybe whining some."

"But Daddy, he looks so cold and so lost. If we don't take him . . ." Everyone knew what happened to stray mongrels: a few days in the Repository, and then any creature not claimed would be sent off to a chattel farm. It might have eight or nine days in the Repository if it was lucky—animals turned in on the weekend were not shipped out the first Monday. But what were the chances of a snub-nosed little creature like this one being claimed? Her father could not in all honesty imagine that they would be high.

"But Daddy, I told him . . . I shouldn't have, but I did . . . I told him he'd be safe, I would take care of him. It was a promise."

Naomi had said the words before she even knew she was going to make them up. And it never crossed her daddy's mind to doubt her; Zayne wasn't good at reading truth and lies. At some level he shrank from this little male animal, cute as it might be. That there was no son of his in the household may have had more to do with his feelings than he would have liked to admit, even to himself—there were shadows there that it was sometimes best to stay away from. Sometimes it was best to stay in the light, with the pure bright colors. But he knew it wouldn't do to start being subtle with a child about promises. You couldn't start splitting hairs about how a promise might not count as quite the same thing if you weren't in a position properly to make the promise. And he couldn't admonish her for letting her feelings get away from her, not when the feelings in question were ones of warmth and generosity. Most of all he couldn't bring himself to argue to her that promises didn't count if they weren't heard and understood, that a bedraggled little mongrel probably could not have understood a word she'd said anyway. All that might be true, but none of it felt like something he could say just now. What he loved most in his daughter was what had made her say just the sort of thing she had said to this creature. The immediacy of her and of how she forged ahead, shining bright, she was like a cadmium yellow but with some ore within it, some hard but precious metal was part of the brightness in her. Zayne wanted to reach out and bring his daughter into his arms and tell her that she had done the bright and good and true thing, and rock her back and forth until it was all better. But perhaps she was getting too big for that now. And things could not be made better that way, he knew that. Still, he started a bit awkwardly to wrap his arms around her. "Your mother . . . ," he began, and then again, "It's the middle of the night, Naomi. And it's freezing." He had suddenly begun to feel the cold—it must be much more of a chill for his daughter's little bones. "Come on back inside; we'll sleep on this and talk it over with your mother in the morning. It's just not something that—"

"But we can't just leave him here Daddy!" Zayne noticed that Naomi called it a "he." Could there be something just the tiniest bit . . . no, "manipulative" couldn't be the right word, he couldn't bring himself to think that, just something very directed in the way she wielded her feelings into words. Maybe that was it. He kept himself from glancing any more at the shivering thing on the corner of the veranda. But Naomi kept looking, and in a moment she saw the piece of paper safety-pinned onto Sam's coverall. She could see there was writing on it. "Look, Daddy, there's a message!" She patted Sam's arm with cautious affection as she undid the pin. Then she passed the note to her father, who began to read:

Dear Mr. and Mrs. Stinson,

I have seen you around in the neighborhood and I am thinking you are good people.

His name is Sam, and he is a good little one. You will be seeing he is a mongrel, I can't be affording to take care of him any more, not him and the others. Please I am hoping that someone may take care of him, he is good, he will be good, to any good family, I think you are a good family please do this for Sam. I will pray.

Tammy had written that but in fact she did not know how to pray, she had never gone to church or temple, had never been taught. But she had wanted to do something like praying, she thought, and those were the words she had.

"Well," said Zayne heavily. "Well." It was often what he said if something important had happened, or was happening, or might happen. "Your mother would be furious, Naomi, you know that." He couldn't help thinking of Carrie and what she would say. He knew Naomi must have thought it too. Carrie would indeed be furious—at him as well as at their daughter, he did not need to add. And when he thought it through, he could hardly blame her. Again and again Carrie had been the practical one, again and again she had been proven right. They had needed to do this or that or to refrain from doing the other thing if they were to get on, if they were to keep some order in their lives and some sense of responsibility, and every time what she said had been true. You couldn't just act on a whim all the time, on a feeling that might be gone from your mind the next morning in any case. If it hadn't been for Carrie's good sense, they never would have made the move out of Woodstock that had all turned out so well. And she wouldn't have gotten the Springfield job. He'd probably still be frittering away his time, painting sporadically in the attic with nothing to show for it but the pictures themselves. The show next month would be at the George Billis Gallery in Chelsea. A good gallery, not one of the most famous, but good, really very good indeed. That would be his fifth solo show, his third in New York.

"We can't just leave him here. We can't, Daddy. He'll . . ."

"He's not going to freeze between now and nine A.M." Zayne could not help sounding a little testy; she was gaining ground. "I will talk to your mother—we will talk to your mother. But it's not something we can decide in a split second. And it's absolutely not something that can be decided without your mother!"

"She won't mind, Daddy, she won't, not if we bring him inside just for now, if we tell her that's what we've done, if we tell her it's just for now. She cares too, I know she does," Naomi added, hesitantly trying out defiance.

"Well, perhaps we could give him a space by the furnace where he could curl up for a few hours. I suppose there would be no great harm in that. But it can't be that we're keeping him. Definitely not, not without . . . not unless . . ."

Sam could not understand the words, but he could see their faces, he could see they would be bringing him inside, he could see that little Naomi was persuading her daddy to give in. It was strange how people dealt with him, now that he was not the lowest member of a family of poor humans, but something else, something a notch lower than that. It seemed they could talk on and on about him with him right there, and never so much as glance in his direction. But they were good people, he could see that, these were not uncaring people. He did not resent how they looked past him. It interested him, that was all, in the way that such things will interest people even when they are very small, very young, and have no words for the ways humans look at each other and look away from each other, and what they mean. But sometimes little creatures know things that they have no words for.

Sam was not crying now. He would not cry anymore, he thought to himself, crying could be something he would keep for when you had to be staying and staying in the out of doors, in the cold, that was where it belonged. And they were going to bring him inside, he knew they were, he really knew it. But couldn't they just hurry a bit? It would be so good to be warm, to be warm through and through.

"Come, little one." The girl had finally turned to him. "You're going to come with me now. You can't be in my room, not yet, anyway, 'cause that's what Daddy says and Mommy except she's not saying yet." She took the creature's hand, which was not entirely easy because of how Sam wanted to keep his blankets wrapped around him as he moved, and Naomi wanted to hold her blankie too. But one way or another they shuffled down to the basement. Zayne laid out a couple of old steamer rugs and the creature lay on top of those, his own blankets still wrapped around him. They said soothing things, especially the girl, and they brought an electric heater into the room and set it up not far away. You would think it would be warm with the furnace right there, but even when the furnace was on it seemed it would send the heat everywhere except the furnace room; on the basement floor it could get very cold, Naomi said to him, not as cold as the veranda, for goodness' sake, but still much too cold to be comfortable. But with the heater that should all be all right. And they didn't have any food for mongrels, they had never had a mongrel, they would get some in the morning so that even if this was just a temporary stop the creature would have a full belly when it went to a permanent home. Zayne did not let himself think of what would await a creature if it were not claimed from the Repositories. He and Naomi made warm noises as they fussed about him a little more, and then they made it dark and Sam pulled his knees right up almost to his chin, he missed his mother so much so much, where was she, *Oh Mommy Mommy I love you I didn't mean to do whatever I did, please don't leave me, Mommy my mommy, I know you are my mommy*, the things that went through his mind were like pain, it was so dark.

Of course they did not decide in the morning to send Sam away; Tammy had guessed right. But it was quite an argument, perhaps the biggest argument in the family's little history. The flames never got out of control. The Stinsons were not that kind of people; that sort of thing was just not in their background. But this time their words took on the kind of heat that you can only get with a hardwood fire, or with coal, a dense heat that could go on and on and on.

"Zayne, we have talked this over in the past."

"Well," Zayne began, but he went no further. They were in the kitchen; Carrie had been dicing carrots when it all came out.

"You and I have talked it over. Several times. And we have talked it over with Naomi too. Also several times." Carrie glanced at her daughter. "This is not the way things are done in this family, Zayne, this is simply not going to happen." He was doing this more and more often, going ahead with something without any consultation, getting their daughter onside with whatever it was he wanted, going against what they had agreed on together as parents and then trying to wheedle his way through it. Why couldn't he be open about things? Have it out with her if need be, but do it beforehand, not like this with Naomi right there. But over the course of a half hour, an hour, two hours, Zayne's dogged patience and the tears that welled periodically in Naomi's eyes wore Carrie down. She was a practical woman, a practical parent, and she was not a heartless one. Even those who had watched Carrie grate against the world like sandpaper—most of whom had felt the abrasiveness themselves at one time or another—would be quick to acknowledge that she was far from heartless. Many would sometimes feel uncertain what she might be capable of, but never for a moment did any of them doubt that her flaws flowed from the determination of a too-passionate heart, not from cruelty or calculation. But her intelligence was never disengaged, as it so often is in the minds of passionate people. She had always acknowledged that life could be unpredictable, that sometimes you had to make unexpected accommodations. Evidently this was one of those times. And perhaps it could be turned to good account after all.

"If you've done something you shouldn't have in life, Naomi, what has to happen?"

"You have to try to make up for it somehow, Mommy."

"And you've done something you shouldn't have, haven't you?"

More than Naomi it was Zayne who had done something he shouldn't have, Carrie knew that perfectly well, but she was starting to think it was too late to get him to change his ways. At least she could try to instill better sense into her daughter. It was a matter of consistency, and of trust too, not just one of honesty.

"Yes, Mommy."

"What *is* the thing you shouldn't have done, Naomi? I want to be sure you understand this." The girl stood awkwardly by the refrigerator. Zayne was off to one side, his fingers drumming ever so lightly on the stone countertop, lightly but incessantly. He backed a little farther away from the other two. He knew that Carrie had to be allowed her moment, had to be allowed to show just how fully she had regained control. Perhaps she had to be allowed to make the child suffer and fade a little bit. To be allowed to make Zayne suffer and fade a little bit too, fade to gray, a lampblack and ivory gray, maybe, or maybe a Payne's gray, you could make a little joke but it wasn't joking time. It would not do to let Carrie see him flinch, he thought; if he backed away just a little bit she would not be able to see anything like that. Not back so far that he was really out of the way, not so far that Naomi wouldn't still be able to see him in the room, see him and know that he would protect her. Just a little bit out of the way, so Carrie would not keep glancing toward him in that way, would not keep thinking of him as part of the problem.

"I went against what we had agreed, Mommy, what we had all agreed. As a family." Naomi fought back her tears as she grasped at the words, trying to remember the words that Mommy had used so she could use those words too, the very same ones.

"And what else?"

"I made a promise. A promise that I couldn't keep." Naomi would make it be in her power, she resolved right then and there, she would make it be in her power to keep all the promises that deserved to be made, to do good things for all the creatures that needed good things done for them, all of them everywhere. For they were good, most of them were, really, how could they be anything but good?

". . . And are you going to make a promise now?" Naomi had missed the first of her mother's words, she would have to make a stab at answering blindly, but maybe she could guess, maybe she could guess it right.

"Yes, Mommy."

"And what are you going to promise to do?"

"I'm going to promise to take care of hit without fail." She had almost said *him*, but Mommy didn't seem to notice, it was going to be all right, if she just followed all the words she wouldn't trip up.

"You're going to feed it every day, twice a day?" A part of Carrie really hated to do this. It was cruel, really, but if you didn't lay things out clearly at the start, that was when you'd get trouble. For the sake of Naomi as well as for the creature itself, it really was important to do this. A few years ago Carrie might have relied on Zayne to help instill some sense of responsibility in the child, after all he was home most of the time, Carrie was the one who put in the hours at work, not crazy hours but enough to bring in the good salary they all depended on. Maybe this Billis show in Chelsea would be different, but the record so far showed you couldn't count on Zayne on the money side of things. Yet somehow it still fell to her to make things work at home. It wasn't a matter of hours, she knew Zayne put in a lot of time with Naomi, *quality time* the expression used to be, and it wasn't a matter of work around the house either, they both did their share of the chores. It was a question of attitude. But Zayne wouldn't change, she had finally come to see that clearly the past year or two, see that the same soft fiber that made him so amiable, so pliable, and so able to feel nothing but color when he wanted to, so able to push everything else off to the side while the glazed alizarin or the smooth cerulean flowed through him and onto the canvas with a purity that used to make her gasp, that same soft fiber wouldn't ever harden, there would never be a spine of responsibility, a firm sense of how you had to lead your life, how you had to bring up your children. Oh, he had the social graces all right, the conventions of politeness and the charm, he was always well behaved in the ways that Carrie didn't give a damn about. Her parents had tried to instill those attributes in her but she had known even as a ten-year-old what it was that really mattered—hard work, a sense of responsibility, real things. It was up to her to teach her daughter those things, to make it clear as could be. If she didn't, everything would get sopped up by the soft, warm, pastel-colored sponge that was life when Zayne was running the show. There was nothing about any of this that Carrie liked. But she knew what Zayne would never be able to know, that the people who make the world go round, the people you can count on, sometimes have to do things they don't like. And her daughter was going to learn that too. If there was one thing Carrie was determined about, it was that.

"Yes, Mother."

"And not let it eat too much or eat the wrong things?"

"No, Mother."

"And you're going to make sure it gets enough exercise?"

"Yes, Mother."

"And you're going to train it." The questions had become statements. "Even a well-behaved mongrel is an imposition on a household, Naomi, you have to understand that. A big imposition. If it's not trained properly it will just be impossible. And if that's the case, there's no way we're keeping it. No way at all. Is that understood?"

"Yes, Mother, I understand."

"Very well. I want you to tell your father and me how sorry you are, and I want to hear you make that promise."

Zayne had no desire whatsoever to hear his daughter make any such promise, but he had even less desire to put himself in Carrie's path just now. When he and Carrie had first met he had found it so refreshing to find someone with a few rough edges, the sort of rough edges he associated with an energy and a drive that floated free of the constraints of social class and of social convention. Had it been inevitable that the energy would come to seem too hard, sharp and steely gray, almost ruthless? That the rough edges would come to seem a little like crudeness? Zayne did not know if there really had been an inevitability to it, but he was all too aware of the degree to which he was complicit in what had happened. That was the word he used to himself, *complicit*. They were all dependent on her, and on her drive, and on the income it brought in for the household, the comforts, the vacations. It wasn't just a matter of finding the courage to resist; when Carrie took a stand like this, he questioned if he had the right to resist.

Broderick, many years later

I STARTED EARLIER to tell you something of the history of the mongrels and of the chattels—and, before that, of the farm animals. I'm going to carry on in that vein now, as I will continue doing here and there throughout these pages. I guess I should make clear, though, that if none of that interests you—if what you really want is to find out about Sam and Naomi, find out how it ends and not hear all the whatnot about politics and the rest of it—that's perfectly all right. You should feel entirely free to skip right over these sections. I know you can get the rest elsewhere. And some of you, of course, may already know the historical background very well. Nonetheless, I can't help stepping in to fill in the gaps for those who may be interested.

When the meat animals and the meat birds and almost all the fish species that humans had consumed died out, there was a great deal of hand-wringing, of course, and widespread recognition that maybe, just maybe, our own behavior had had something to do with it, that the diseases wouldn't have spread so quickly if the creatures hadn't been packed thousands upon thousands together in feedlots or in dark and poorly ventilated sheds,* if science hadn't been taken so aggressively to extremes to make each carcass uniformly productive, if the number of species hadn't been so greatly reduced, in turn drastically reducing resistance to disease, or if antibiotics hadn't been used so frequently and so thoughtlessly, quietly paving the way for the pandemics. Oh, people

---

*Many of the same issues—the overuse of antibiotics lowering resistance to disease, the overcrowding facilitating the spread of disease—also applied to fish farms, which over the course of the late twentieth and early twenty-first centuries had come to provide almost all the fish consumed by humans; overfishing had by 2030 or thereabouts devastated the wild stocks.

had realized it, all right, some people anyway, but probably no more than a small minority. Just as it is only a small minority nowadays who seem to realize that society is making the same mistakes all over again. Maybe if the choice had been starkly in front of people, they wouldn't have taken the road they did. But, of course, a clear choice was never right there at any one moment in time, there was the long transition, forty, fifty years of it. And everything seemed to happen disconnectedly; there were no great moments of choice at any point in time, no election campaigns charged with passion over these issues, no series of referendums. On the one hand was the realization that humans would need protein and other nutrients to replace what we had been getting from all the chicken and fish and pork and beef. Soy and other legumes were the obvious candidates, but right at the time of the great extinctions it was striking how many articles and seescreen features started to appear on the dangers of soy, on how too much soy could rot your liver or destroy your joints, or make you persistently enervated and depressed. It all seemed to have a good deal of credibility, and there was just too much of it to ignore.* People ate

*The campaign against soy, driven largely by parties with a vested interest in seeing the meat and dairy industries prosper, has an extraordinarily long history. Even in the very early years of the twenty-first century scare articles on "the dangers of soy" were widely disseminated. But if you looked into matters closely you would inevitably find that that the scare-mongering lacked scientific support. To be sure, some dangers were associated with the soy monocultures that genetic engineering was bringing about; when Monsanto and the other agribusiness giants of the day created monoculture soybeans, many scientists felt that they had created a truly dangerous situation. But whatever dangers there were stemmed from the process of genetic modification and the principle of monoculture, not from anything specific to soy. Genetically modified monoculture canola and genetically modified monoculture corn were at least as bad. If those scientists were right, then *stay away from genetically modified crops* was the lesson to be learned, not *stay away from soy*. Another area of contention was infant formula. Numerous studies suggested that soy-based infant formulas did not provide everything a baby needed. But that had to do not with soy per se but with infant formula, any infant formula. Study after study showed that breast milk was best. Unless you planned on feeding your baby nothing but soy formula (almost as bad an idea as feeding it nothing but cow's milk formula) you had nothing to fear from soy. And a lot to gain from it: study after study also showed that a soy-rich vegetarian diet was at least as healthy as a diet rich in meat and dairy products, that vegetarians had better calcium balance and stronger bones, healthier levels of other essential minerals, a lower incidence of heart disease, a lower incidence of cancer, fewer birth defects

soy, of course, and many were astonished to discover how it could be transformed—not only transformed into a variety of incarnations unique unto themselves, but also miraculously transformed so as to imitate with uncanny similitude almost any meat dish they could remember. So yes, people ate soy, and were often surprised to find they enjoyed it. But with all the negative publicity, increasingly they came to tell themselves (and tell their friends and relatives too) that they were eating soy "for the time being," and that no doubt alternatives would come along; it really was remarkable what science could do. After a few years, though, science had done nothing remarkable by way of discovering a "new meat," and all the while had seemed to be discovering more and more negative things about soy and the way it could affect human health. Quite naturally, anxiety levels began to rise. More and more people began to urge that we seek out new sources of protein, as well as new sources of various minerals and other nutrients that were widely believed to be in short supply (but that in fact were for the most part readily available in ample quantities in a wide variety of vegetables and legumes). That went on for some years without any suggestion of panic, and despite their anxiety people did seem to understand intuitively that no industry and no government could, overnight, solve problems as great as those created by the great extinctions.

And on the economic side of things: there was for a long, long time an economic depression, of course, and certainly that made a very great difference to the way things turned out. The meat processors, the ranchers,

---

in their offspring, and improved cognitive function. Nor, despite widespread rumors to the contrary, was there anything to suggest that soy would reduce the male libido, or give males "feminine" characteristics. To be sure, a 2008 Harvard study had pointed to reduced sperm counts in obese white males who were also heavy consumers of soy—but even in that group sperm counts remained within the normal range, and the doctor who had conducted the study (and whose other studies included work on the health benefits of replacing animal sources of protein with vegetable sources) emphasized that people should not worry about whether they were "eating too much soy." Sperm counts among males in the developed world did decline significantly in the late twentieth and early twenty-first centuries—but as we now know, that had to do primarily with increases in their ingestion of chemicals of the sort found in factory-farmed products of all sorts; most males would have been far more fertile had their diet been an organic vegetarian one—or had they consumed free-range rather than factory-farmed meat and dairy products.

the fast-food operations—in every sector, vast companies either went under or were forced to transform themselves to deal with the shock. With so many companies on the ropes, and so many people unemployed, the strain on the public purse was enormous. From all sides voices brayed against any cutbacks in funding for this, that, and the other good cause. But it was clear that quite a few things had to give if a complete collapse of government services was to be avoided. Some even thought there was some danger of society itself suffering a complete collapse. In such a climate it was entirely understandable that a sea change in attitudes would sweep through society. And when the change came it was stronger, for example, than had been most of the waves of anti-immigrant or race-based feeling that had periodically swept through most nations in earlier times. Much stronger. White people used to hate the thought of a black person touching the water they swam in; Christians and Muslims had for long periods thought of each other as less than fully human—and thought of Jews as lower still. The reaction against mongrels (more accurately I should say, in order to avoid anachronism, the reaction against the various subgroups that are now classed together as mongrels) might be compared to those sorts of feelings in earlier eras. Certainly many began to think of mongrels as less than fully human—and before long, as not human at all. To more and more people the very idea of giving jobs, or government grants, or hospital beds to mongrels was like the idea of giving such things to cows or pigs in an earlier era. How could one justify lavishing attention on such creatures when too little attention was being paid to humans who needed help?

Very clearly it was not a situation that could be sustained, and within a few years of the great extinctions things had begun to change very significantly. People in respectable circles never said publicly that people had to come first and that those creatures which weren't really human could not continue to receive all the same services, all the same benefits as humans did. But they said it among themselves, and friends talked to friends. And in some of the more populist media, columnists and commentators did begin to say such things publicly; they were not reprimanded for doing so, and letters and phone calls ran heavily in their favor. That was enough to tip the scales. Soon the families of mongrels began to be told more and more often that, in view of the backlog, it was just impossible to say when some family member who needed it might get a bed at the hospital, for example, or a date for cardiac surgery. Mongrels, as they were coming generally to be called, could for a time still get the existing drugs and treatments, but as soon as new ones were developed it seemed that more insurance plans (government run as well as private) were excluding mongrels from coverage. And before long the "grandfathered" coverage began to lapse in one jurisdiction after another.

Soon the average life expectancy for a mongrel was no longer forty or fifty years, or even twenty-five; it had dropped to levels as low as had been the norm in the 1920s.

Parental attitudes changed too—that may have been the biggest thing. People became less willing or able to put in the time required to raise one that needed a lot of special attention. Or, in a society increasingly divided between rich and poor, to put up the money. Understandably then, if a mongrel arrived it would more and more frequently be put up for adoption, and more and more frequently no one would wish to adopt it. Then it would be put into a public facility, of course—but, as people quickly came to realize, you couldn't use a public facility such as a hospital or a residential school for a purpose like that. That would be an absurd drain on the public purse, on the pocketbooks of taxpayers who worked to earn their dollars and who would not stand to see them spent except in the most useful and productive ways. You wouldn't want society to be inhumane, but you had to be realistic, just as societies from the beginning of time had been forced to be realistic. The Inuit, goodness knows, were famous for their tradition of quietly leaving defectives literally out in the cold, and throughout history other societies had done the same thing, whether literally or metaphorically, with the same results.

Compared to the way those other societies had behaved, our own behavior seemed quite benign. The foster dormitories for mongrels—now called "Repositories" in most North American jurisdictions—simply began to make mongrels available to families on a very different basis than they had been a generation earlier. It was asserted on a variety of fronts that the loss of dogs and of cats was in its way as great a loss to humanity as that of beef or pork or cod or chicken, some said an even greater loss. The loss of meat had allegedly left a yawning gap in human nutrition—at least in rich countries. The gap left by the loss of dogs and cats was not one of nutrition (except in China, Vietnam, and a handful of other

Southeast Asian nations, where the population had traditionally been far less discriminating as to what constituted edible flesh than the population was in Britain or North America—or, for that matter, than it was in India or Bangladesh, Zambia or Zimbabwe). Rather, to lose a cat or dog was an emotional loss for many families and even more so for many single people, a deeply and profoundly emotional loss.

What was not so quickly realized was how readily the gap might be filled. But as soon as a few of the Repositories began to think of it as a solution to their problem of overcrowding, the idea immediately took off. Almost everyone seemed suddenly to agree that mongrels could look cute, and many discovered that their warmth and their whimpering could be as comforting as that of a Pekinese or a Labrador.

That solved a good deal of the problem, but it turned out to be a problem that kept on growing. As is now generally acknowledged in the scientific community, certain airborne particulates* had become steadily more widespread through the twenty-first century, especially following the spread of silicon technology in the late 1900s. The line tracking this development mapped almost precisely onto the line that tracked the increase in the birth of mongrels over the same period. There was for a long time no conclusive proof that the connection was causal. And no one properly understood the mechanism involved. But there clearly *was* a connection; anyone who was at all informed could be in no doubt that a connection existed, that something was going horribly wrong.† In the 1980s there had been 1 mongrel birth for every 300 to 400 human births,‡ in 2020 the ratio had risen to 1 in 150, and by 2050 to 1 in 60. (These increases at first came despite modest improvements in the degree to which prenatal

---

*This was the name that gained currency in the early twenty-first century after a variety of interested parties lobbied successfully against the use of the term *pollutants*.

†The consensus view in the scientific community was that you could draw a fair parallel between knowledge at that time of a silicon-mongrel connection and knowledge in the 1960s of a smoking–lung cancer connection.

‡Aggregate statistics are used here, of course, so as to compare like to like; again, the modern category of mongrel brings together a large number of categories that in the twentieth and early twenty-first centuries were classified as distinct.

screening could identify certain high-risk pregnancies.*) Even before the great extinctions, in other words, there had been a far greater number of mongrels putting pressure on the system. Even greater pressure than would otherwise have been the case, since the capabilities of "the new mongrels" were almost always more severely limited than had been the case with mongrels of earlier eras. Was that merely the result of their receiving fewer of society's scarce resources? Had there been the resources to research the question thoroughly, that might have been made clear. Understandably enough, the priorities of science and of society increasingly lay elsewhere; keeping pace with the needs of human beings was enough to stretch what resources there were to the limit.

But the problem of the "new mongrels" refused to go away, however much it was ignored. The numbers—both the raw numbers and the percentages—just kept on rising. In the immediate wake of the great extinctions the ratio of mongrel to human births rose to one in thirty, then one in fifteen; not long after that the ratio was approaching one in five. It became impossible to ignore the size of the problem, impossible to think of any way to address it without implementing radical changes. But there was no political constituency that would openly support radical change. For that reason radical change happened over the course of decades rather than weeks or months. And it happened with virtually no acknowledgment of the degree to which it *was* in fact radical. One step was a growing consensus that, once a mongrel suffered from cardiac disease or chronic infection of a serious nature, it would be doing the creature no kindness to try to draw out its life unnecessarily. Rather than asking a mongrel of this sort to live out the rest of its short lifespan in pain, was it not kinder to bring its life to a gentle end?

---

*The detection of various abnormalities using ultrasound had enabled doctors from the mid-1990s onward to identify many fetuses with a higher than normal risk of being born with certain defects, and amniocentesis could often then provide a reliable diagnosis. But amniocentesis carried with it some risk to the fetus (as well as entailing a good deal of expense); there could be numerous dilemmas, medical as well as ethical. And as the twenty-first century wore on, of course, ultrasound and associated technologies inexplicably started to become less and less reliable as predictive tools. That development has baffled medical and veterinary science now for the better part of a century.

It came to be generally acknowledged that the answer to such a question could only be in the affirmative, but a heated debate then arose over what further steps needed to be taken. Very quickly the supply of mongrels had come to exceed the demand; it did not seem likely that as many people would ever want pet mongrels as had once wanted Airedales or Siamese. For a brief period a number of cogent voices pointed to a potential connection between the alleged shortage of protein and the evident surplus of mongrels. Given that most of the surplus creatures were already facing an early and far from pleasant conclusion to their lives, these cogent voices plausibly argued that it was merely practical and not in any way cruel to look at the big picture, to see the surplus mongrels not simply as a key part of a large problem, but as a key part of a potential *solution* to that problem. Rather than letting them die often painful deaths due to illness, would it not make sense to harvest a proportion of the mongrel population at a somewhat earlier stage? That would, it was argued, be a win-win situation. It would lead in most cases to a happier end for the mongrels themselves, and certainly it would provide at least a partial solution to what was being seen as a great crisis in nutrition.*

It did not take much of a nudge to tip public opinion into an acceptance of the appropriateness of considering a mongrel-centered solution to the perceived nutrition problem. To be sure, a few dissenting voices were raised. But remarkably quickly, the stage of open debate came to an end. Either no one was sending letters to the editor or calling in comments, or else the editorial staffs had simply stopped publishing and airing the views of dissenters. However it happened, the debate went away surprisingly quickly.

---

*As it happened, this discussion occurred at a time when publicity about the supposed dangers of soy was at a peak. It would not be for another fifteen years that the body of research then being so widely reported began to come into question. Not until much later still would it be revealed that the large meat-processing companies had played a key role in the early funding and dissemination of "research findings" on the dire health hazards of soy. But I suppose it could hardly be expected that at that late stage any such revelation could have had a material effect on people's behavior, any more than the revelation years and years after the fact of the part that the auto industry had played in destroying the early twentieth-century streetcar networks in North American cities had a material effect on people's by then entrenched habit of going everywhere by car.

And then, a year or so after that, it all simply began to happen. There had been no official permission given. But nor was there any clear, legal prohibition in any jurisdiction across North America, federal, state, or provincial; in any country in Asia, Africa, or South America; in Australia, in New Zealand. (In Brussels things were, of course, different; it was not until much later that meat eating began again in the European Union, and then only under regulations far stricter than would ever be approved in America, even after the various tainted-meat scandals.) Not surprisingly, it was among the better-off that the new way of doing things began—particularly among the gourmands, those who valued exquisite taste above all. These were the people who in the old days had found the idea of becoming a vegetarian quite laughable, not because they found such beliefs objectionable on any grounds of principle (though no doubt many of them did), but because they found them to be simply incomprehensible.

The gourmands did not wield the cleaver themselves, of course. Indeed, they did very little to initiate things. Enterprising intermediaries began to offer their services to catering companies, and to wealthy individuals and families, couching their pitch in language that made the whole enterprise seem almost charitable. If the party were to make a substantial donation to the Repository, it would assist the keepers in putting to sleep in humane fashion a creature whose cardiac irregularities indicated it was otherwise likely doomed to a painful end. The prognosis typically made reference to the near inevitability of a mongrel stroke, or of mongrel cardiac arrest. Never just *stroke* or *cardiac arrest*, always *mongrel stroke*, *mongrel cardiac arrest*—just as in the old days it had been, for example, *bovine encephalitis*. (In fact, infection of various sorts rather than either stroke or heart failure was always the leading cause of mongrel death before the meat-packing industry started up again.) Almost as an afterthought it was noted that the donors would have the option of retaining a quarter or a half side for their own consumption. Should the donor wish to exercise that option, the desired amount could be dressed and prepared according to specifications, thereby ensuring a ready supply of protein-rich nourishment to the donor's family for months to come.

Of course the product was not called *mongrel* or *mongrel meat*. Just as in the old days people had distanced themselves from the animals they were eating by calling a cow *beef* and a pig *pork*, so too did they find other

56 · Don LePan

names for mongrel meat.* In North America it became known as *yurn*, in Britain and in Australia as *fland*—though in Britain it was often also referred to as *new mince*, after the most popular ground form. Generally, the names chosen drew attention to the supposed mildness of the product, in its aroma as well as its flavor.

As with almost any new industry, risk takers led the way. The first producers were acutely conscious of the risks involved. These were not limited to the normal business risks: would there be sufficient demand for the new product, would there be unanticipated costs or production problems? There were also significant legal risks. Crucially, the view that no legal prohibition existed against the production and sale of yurn depended on the law being interpreted in such a way as to define mongrels as animals, not as humans.† Generations earlier, mongrels had almost universally been assumed to be human, but no one had thought to say in so many words in

---

*It is interesting that the urge toward name substitution is far from universal. In particular, people seem less squeamish about assigning the name of the animal to what they are eating when the animal is more or less wild (*bison, moose, antelope*) or when the creature being eaten is "lower" than a mammal (*chicken, duck, frog*). Issues of class and of proximity to the animals before they become meat also enter into it. In England following the Norman Conquest, for example, the French names came to be used for animals in the form in which they were eaten (*beef, pork, mutton*), whereas the English names were applied to the animals in the field; the English peasants who raised the animals used their words for the creatures themselves, while the upper-class French used their words for the cooked creatures once they had reached the dining table.

†It is often imagined that the answer to a question such as what constitutes a human person is self-evident, and does not change over time. Yet even a moment's reflection shows this idea to be false. Americans living as chattel slaves held the status of less-than-fully-human animals, as did slaves in the colonies of Britain, France, Spain, and other European nations; in ancient Greece and Rome; in the Mayan and Aztec empires—the list goes on and on. Quite aside from any issue of slavery, many societies of one race have regarded the members of certain other races as nonhuman animals. The lower castes in India and in Japan did not attain full legal status as humans until the latter part of the twentieth century, and even through much of the twenty-first century continued to be treated as lower-order beings. Women have in many cultures been regarded as less than fully human by their male rulers, and in many jurisdictions battles have been waged over whether a fetus is a human or a less-than-human being. And, with more justification, many societies have regarded those born with various defects as thereby lacking fully human status.

any of the relevant statutes, "Someone suffering from Peake's syndrome [or Sellars' dystrophy, or Wilson's disorder, etc.] shall be always deemed to have the legal standing of a person, not that of a non-human animal." Now that such a great change in public perception had occurred and mongrels were widely, even generally, assumed to be less than human, would the courts follow? The same laws remained in place; it was all a matter of interpretation. The pivotal case in the United States, *Collins v. Ella's Delicatessen*, could hardly be said to have been fought on neutral ground. Craig Collins had abandoned the mongrel that his wife had borne him, and had then had second thoughts when his wife died a month later of ongoing complications stemming from the birth. But Collins was an overbearing crank; despite the tragic circumstances, most found it hard to sympathize with him. And Ella, proprietor of a highly popular little deli, was the perfect image of the entrepreneur with a real connection to her neighborhood and a strong conscience, the sort who would always put service to her community above profit. In a six–three vote the Court decided that a mongrel was a non-human animal. Similar cases went the same way in other nations (the highest-profile cases among them were perhaps *Parker v. Glebe Grocers* in Canada and *Crown v. NSW Newtrients* in Australia), and the world moved on.

Once the legal uncertainty had been cleared away, a series of further changes followed in quick succession. The Repositories were obviously not equipped to fulfill the functions of a butcher shop or a meat-packing plant. The necessary facilities were at first provided by former butchers who had been thrown out of work years earlier during the great extinctions, and were now more than willing (for the handsome amounts offered) to refit a garage or a storage shed for the work. It was individuals of this sort who established the new cuts, and adapted old butchers' vocabulary to describe them. As a rule there were fewer points of connection between the names and the specific parts of the carcass than there had been with beef, pork, or chicken. Terms such as *rolled roast* or *circle steak* or *Denver slice* were used in preference to *flank steak*, say, or *shoulder roast*.

Those pioneers played a vital role in giving some shape to the new industry. But they could only do that for as long as the trade itself remained very small, virtually a cottage industry. What quickly became clear was that demand was so high, even at the exorbitant prices that were charged in those early days before the reproductive revolution, that it would not be possible to arrange things along the lines of a cottage industry for long. People who had tasted yurn once at an elegant dinner party or exclusive function at a club wanted to make a donation themselves—a donation that would ensure themselves a quarter- or a half-side of their own. It quickly became *de rigueur* in stylish circles to add at least a yurn appetizer to the menu for any catered event. And some high-end restaurants were willing to pay almost any price for the finest cuts.

It was widely agreed that people had simply been starved of protein-rich nourishment for too long. But the surge in demand was surely also a result of the degree to which the food service industry had been starved of new products, particularly new products that catered to the human weakness for animal fats. In discussing the phenomenon people have said a great deal about protein and little or nothing about fat, though the near addictive properties of animal fats had been widely documented for many decades prior to the great extinctions.*

There can be no question too that the old meat-based industries had a good deal to do with the way in which yurn took off. It turned out that very few of these companies had actually died; the chicken factories and the feedlots and the slaughterhouses had all disappeared, but most of the companies that had operated them had bought into (or merged with) firms in unrelated industries, and had remained very much alive. As Slyson Products and Services, the old Slyson Foods had lived on, as had most of the giants of the industry, in one form or another. Almost immediately they began to set up dozens of small businesses—*maisons de préparation*, they came to be called—to deal, exactly as the name suggested, with the preparation of the product. And for a short time they remained small businesses, even

---

*Of great relevance in many minds to the issue of how protein and animal fat "short-ages" are interpreted is the question of whether or not meat-eating is natural to humans. If the emergence first of homo erectus and then of homo sapiens stemmed from a shift from a vegetable to a meat-based diet, as many still believe, then surely it is natural for us to crave the taste sensations that meat products give us. Natural, and thereby justifiable, so the argument goes. But what if, as other researchers sug-gest, the key development in "making humans human" was the introduction not of meat-eating but of cooking? To my mind these anthropological issues, however inter-esting, have no bearing on the issue of how we should conduct ourselves today.

humane businesses, hiring the butchers who had started in their own garages, running clean and careful shops, making sure they contributed to the community, connected in only the most tenuous and unobtrusive ways with the larger companies planning and funding their growth.

It should hardly have been surprising that the old giants of the meat business would reemerge and do everything they could to feed the growth of the new industry. But it did surprise many that demand for yurn would turn out to be so high, given the product's extraordinary price and extraordinary provenance. Before the time of the reproductive revolution the price charged for yurn was above that charged for caviar. Perhaps the only historical parallel on the price side had been the $500-per-pound prices (equivalent to almost $5,000 per pound in today's money) that Kobe beef had commanded in the late twentieth and early twenty-first centuries.*

If the strong demand for yurn was explicable in the context of the times, things on the supply side were perhaps more surprising. Statistics became increasingly hard to come by, but there could be no doubt that for a remarkable length of time, as the industry grew, there was no supply

---

*If people had thought through the historical comparison a little more fully the new reality might have seemed less surprising. Those long-ago exorbitant prices for Kobe beef stemmed in part from the elaborate care with which the animals had been raised and fed. Even more important, they were rooted in the economics of scarcity, in the import quotas that Japan imposed on beef from abroad, and in the very limited capacity for beef production within Japan itself. For different reasons, the supply of yurn when it was introduced was also very limited. But the structural forces driving demand for luxury goods in the two situations were different. Japan in the late twentieth and early twenty-first centuries was a far more egalitarian society than was the United States—top executives would typically be paid no more than ten times what the average worker was paid, and that put real limits on the discretionary spending power of most of those Japanese who were classed as rich. In the United States, on the other hand, CEO "executive compensation" (as it rather oddly came to be called) was even then typically one hundred or two hundred times that of the average worker. And those exorbitant compensation levels continued to rise throughout the twenty-first century, as the divide between rich and poor in America grew ever wider. When that side of the equation is recalled, it should be little wonder that luxury goods in general were able to command unprecedented prices in late twenty-first-century America—and that yurn in particular was from the moment of its introduction able to command prices in America that were substantially higher (even in inflation-adjusted currency) than the top prices Kobe beef had commanded a century or so earlier.

problem. No matter how many *maisons de préparation* sprouted up, there seemed to be enough product to keep them operating at something close to capacity. As previously cited, the ratio of mongrel births to human births rose to remarkably high levels. But it was also believed that the rate was *bound* to level off—which the demand for yurn showed no sign of doing. It began to strike many people that society's interests would be well served if fewer mothers—or perhaps I had better say fewer parents, for fathers were becoming more and more involved in these decisions—if fewer parents decided to abort a mongrel rather than carrying it through to term. More and more, opinion makers started to be of the view that these very personal decisions also had very real implications for the nourishment of society at large. For many years the Repositories had provided hatches through which newly born mongrels could be dropped off anonymously; there was already no need to endure the awkwardness or humiliation of having given birth to a creature of that sort. But the reality was that unless people were given good reasons to do otherwise, only those implacably opposed to abortion would carry a creature to term once they discovered it to be mongrel rather than human. And while screening had started to become less effective,* in these early days it was still widely relied on. If it was clearly advisable from a public-policy point of view for a substantial percentage of those who were pregnant to carry mongrel fetuses to term, there would have to be incentives; that much was clear.

It all developed as markets often do, in an uneven and somewhat makeshift fashion at first, then becoming better and better organized, less susceptible to large fluctuations in price. The mechanism itself was very simple. Once you had established that you were going to give birth to a mongrel rather than a human, you chose either to abort it or to carry it to term. In the latter case there were some, of course, who would keep their mongrels as household pets. But once the system of incentives became established, the common practice soon became to make arrangements with one of the clinics associated with the *maisons de préparation*. One would never become wealthy from what one would receive as an "honorarium" after one had delivered, and for that reason it was unheard

---

*Cf. footnote on page 53.

of for well-educated or wealthy women (or, indeed, middle-class women) to take this route. But a woman working in a menial job could often top up her earnings for a year by 15 percent—in some cases even 20 or 30 percent. That might not sound like a great deal when you consider the extraordinary amount of time and inconvenience involved, but in fact it did make an appreciable difference for many.* Eventually, then, both supply and demand came into equilibrium and the whole thing worked; a moment came when the system seemed firmly to have been locked into place.

But I have no doubt spent far too long on the history and the economics— the big picture—when I know what many of you are interested in is the narrative of individual lives. Let me turn you back to the manuscript and the story of what happened with Sam, and with Naomi.

• •

For perhaps a month Sam kept his place by the furnace. For the first week Carrie acted distant, even a little frosty, toward him. It was hard for her not to feel that something a little like betrayal had happened. Zayne had known perfectly well her reasons for not wanting a pet mongrel, had known *all* her reasons, even the ones they had agreed never to speak of. And now he had gone ahead and—but you had to move forward, she would not keep dwelling on that.

And she did not dwell on it. Before long she began to soften noticeably toward Sam. It wasn't just that she was accepting his presence; she began to feel genuine affection for him. Of course it was hard not to soften toward a creature that had Sammy's disposition. He was always smiling, always friendly, always trying to help. But

---

*Of course such payments were far from being enough to enable these low-income women, however important they might be to the creation of the product, also to be numbered among its consumers. It was acknowledged, though, that pregnant women require more protein in their diets than do other humans, and honest efforts were made to educate the women on these nutritional matters and to point out to them that, no matter what the advertisements for yurn in the fancy women's magazines might claim, in cases such as their own the required amounts—and a good deal more—of protein and other nutrients could readily be obtained through the consumption of significant amounts of nuts or soy or other legumes.

he was careful never to try too hard to help, or to get in your way when you were trying to concentrate on something. (For the first two weeks he had stayed pretty well clear of Carrie, and that surely had helped.)

Naomi did everything she had been asked to do, and a good deal more. She took Sam for his walks, she made sure he always had food and water, she washed his coverall every second day, she even made sure his little area by the furnace was neat as could be. Those things were sort of for Sam but mostly they were for the sake of her mother and for the sake of learning responsibility, and for all the big things outside of herself. The things that were for Sam and Sam only were a floppy stuffed penguin that her aunt and uncle had given her, she loved it but not so much as she once had loved it. Sam loved it more. Also a big box of crayons. He loved that too, and she had enough crayons anyway, too many even. Also three stones and pebbles from her collection, including one of her pink striped ones, they were her favorites. Also two books, of course he couldn't read or understand words properly, but maybe he could sort of understand if there were pictures. They were two of her favorites, one was *Where the Wild Things Are*, one was *Winnie the Pooh*; she had been given two copies of each of them at different times (her aunts and uncles were always giving her things she had already) so that didn't count as a proper gift to Sam, but you could see he liked it, liked both of them and that they were his very own. Any creature could love pictures, especially of Piglet, Naomi thought, and of Pooh Bear, she would find a way to get him his own bear but for now they could share, he could snuggle her teddy, he liked that, it was so soft and friendly, and Naomi snuggled Sam too. It was all right to do that with a mongrel, it wasn't like with a mommy where you could have too much hugging; like her mommy said, you can't be hugging and all touchy-feely all the time, that wasn't what life was all about, but with a mongrel it was different. Probably they needed more love than human children did, that might be it, Naomi was thinking, she could give little Sam all he needed maybe, or maybe not all but a lot, she would try so hard.

And he hugged her in return, and loved her, she thought of it as holding him but really he was holding her too, and loving her too.

He was always darting glances at her to see if she was happy, what could he do to make her happy? She had saved him, he sensed that through and through, and he was determined not to cry in front of her, people got upset if you cried and he never did, he always made himself wait if he was feeling the sadness coming, wait until she had left him, had turned out the light and shut the door. Then it was all right to cry, that was the all-right time. But all that changed after the first few months when Naomi had gotten permission from her mommy and her daddy to bring him upstairs at night, to let him have his space with his blankets at the foot of her bed. It was such a good change but when the sadness came in the dark he could not hide his tears, not one night especially, and he sobbed and sobbed and sobbed and she held him and she rocked him gently over and over and he could see she kept saying soft things; that was the only time, though, all the other times he kept it inside him or the sounds were just little and Naomi was sleeping.

He watched her mouth. Over and over he watched her mouth. And the things she did with her mouth. She did them slowly, most of time anyway she did them slowly, she would point at the little figure running with the big red circle, *baa-loon* she would say, the tip of her finger on the big red circle, *baa-loon*, and then with her finger pointing to the little one, *pi-*, *pi-*, *pig-let*, and something kept happening in his brain as he watched her, as she held him close under the covers; she was not supposed to let him come under the covers, but Mommy never caught her, never, she only did it when she knew her mommy was all busy somewhere else. Any time Carrie would come in, there Sam would be, good as gold at the foot of the bed, just where he was supposed to be.

Sometimes Naomi would also watch him when he was like that. She would not just give him a quick glance, like Mommy did, and a little smile to show she approved of how everything was working out and how she wasn't angry not even a little bit, but Naomi knew that wasn't quite true, knew from the sharp looks that Mommy looked when she looked at Sam that she still had some strange feeling about him, that was why they had to be so careful, always Naomi would look at Sam for long, long times when he was sleeping. And for short times when he was awake but he wasn't looking at her, sometimes when he was doing something else, busy with something, thinking about something. She looked at him and she tried to see.

And the more Naomi looked at him the more she would wonder how it worked inside him. How different was he? How different were all of them, the mongrels? Maybe they weren't really that different at all, maybe they could think things and feel things almost as we can. Well, *feel* things, that much she felt sure about, they could feel almost the way that humans did, maybe more than some humans. Preston, the Carsons' mongrel, was just as much filled with feeling as most humans, you could see it, and think of Mr. Carson, who never seemed to feel for anyone but himself. You could tell Preston felt sad when bad things happened to him or were done to him by Mr. Carson, and you could tell he felt happy when he had a new mongrel toy or the sun came through the window and shone through the floating dust in the air. But mostly you could tell he felt sad, the same sort of sad as when Sandy the little Carson child hurt his arm or got made fun of by the Ransom boys down the street. You could see that Preston's sad was just like Sandy's sad, except there was more of it. Mongrels could feel all right, Naomi knew that right as rain, and there were thoughts inside them too, thousands of thoughts, of course there were. Maybe they could even talk, talk *properly*, maybe if you really tried—because no one *did e*ver try, not really, Naomi was sure of that. Maybe you could make words form inside their little heads and come out, proper words. Koko the gorilla and Washoe the chimpanzee had learned sign language, and they had proven that even a bird could talk! Naomi had read about Alex, Alex the African gray from long ago, and about all the African grays they had worked with after Alex, there was a book at the library, people didn't have the money to do learning like that with birds, it said, but still, the knowing was there. Alex had been just a parrot but he didn't just parrot things. *Parroting*, that was the word people used when there was only sound and no thought, but with Alex there had been thought, Dr. Pepperberg had taught him dozens and dozens of words. He had been able to make up whole sentences, to count, to tell you what color something was. And when he had gone into his birdcage for the night on what turned out to be his last night Alex had said to her, to Dr. Pepperberg that was, "You be good, see you tomorrow, I love you." But he never did, he died in the night. He had been old, thirty-one years old, Naomi remembered it all from the story book of true stories. So she knew perfectly well that animals could talk, some of them anyway, and her mommy and daddy and Mr. Simon at school couldn't tell her any different; she *knew*! And for sure some mongrels could say some things as well as understand things, they were sort of animals but sort of like humans too. They just hadn't been taught to do things; maybe she could be a teacher.

That was part of why Naomi kept showing Sam her books, not just the two that were his now, but a lot of them. She would keep skittering over to her bookshelf, the one that held all the big books from when she had been little, the picture books. And a moment later she would have him beside her all snug on the bed or on the sofa and they would be turning the pages together. In and out of weeks and almost over a year, that was how time passed where the wild things were, and maybe Naomi was living in a storybook too, almost over a year had gone by, maybe more, and still nothing seemed to make sense to Sam, almost nothing anyway, none of the sounds would make sense to him, maybe it was dreaming to think that things would make sense for him but she kept thinking that as time kept stretching a key would turn and all the things would be open to him and make sense for him when she found the key. She would keep working at it, she would find a way to make him put the sounds together, just like her mommy had said, you have to keep working at things if you want them to happen. Sam wouldn't be able to hear the sounds until Naomi could find a way to help him put them together, maybe it was important for him to see her making the sounds too. With every page she would turn to him, making sure he could see the big slow movements she made with her lips and her cheeks and her tongue. "Aaah," she read out from under the picture of the tongue depressor. No, that wouldn't mean a lot to him, the veterinarian didn't make mongrels open their mouths like she did with humans, maybe the next page was better, "*Baa*," she read from under the picture of the sheep. That was simpler than *Piglet* or *balloon*. He had never seen a sheep, any more than she had—now people knew them only from books and old films, but everyone still knew the sound that sheep were supposed to have made. "Just look at me," she said, and she gestured and then, with his eyes fixed on her, she said again and again and again, "*Baa, Baa, Baa,*" very slowly, very clearly, her lips parting each time as she exaggerated the sounds. She could see him pressing his little lips together and popping them apart: together, apart, together, apart, trying so hard to mimic her. And then it came. A little popping sound, it might have been more a *p* than a *b* but it was there, she could hear it, there was no doubt. She could do it, they could do it together, it was wonderful, wonderful, wonderful, and maybe they would even be special friends, but for now it was just that her heart was filled with joy. This was no time to stop, though, she squeezed his shoulder a little bit as she turned the page and smiled before she began to form another sound, oh so slowly and so large, with her mouth. "Caa," she read from under the picture of the toy car, "caa," "caa," and then all of it, all three letters, "car." But no, she thought, it will be easier for him if I leave off the *r*, everything easy, make everything easy at first, as easy as it can be, maybe even easy will be hard for him. "Look at me, look at my lips, *caa, caa, caa.*" And faithfully there came back an echo, but not of all the sounds, *ah* was all there was, and then *ah*, they would have to keep working, working, working, but it was such good and such happy work.

Broderick, many years later

I SAID A little earlier that the system had seemed to be locked firmly into place. But it is so often just when everyone agrees that something is at its most advanced and most efficient stage (whether for good or for ill) that something further happens, something revolutionary. So it was with mongrels and chattels. Things turned out not to be in their final stage at all, not by a long shot. Of course anyone reading these pages will be aware of the transformation wrought by the great reproductive revolution. That is not the stuff of long-ago history that many have forgotten and many more never bothered to learn; it is the stuff of the living present. For that reason I will do no more than touch upon it here, the great breakthrough that has led to sustainable chattel populations no longer dependent on human reproductive agency.

Research into the reproductive cloning of humans had all but come to a halt in the early twenty-first century. Progress on the cloning of foodstuffs continued on many fronts (though not without controversy), but virtually all authorities refused to permit work on human reproductive cloning.* There were technical issues too. For all the high-profile successes in cloning other mammals, the failure rate had remained discouragingly high—as had the cost. The scientific breakthroughs of the past generation in developing methods of cloning chattels with ever increasing efficiency and at ever lower expense are, of course, well known. But what made them possible at a fundamental level, I would argue, was the realization

---

*Even Dr. Samuel Wood, who with his colleague Andrew French succeeded in 2008 in cloning five mature human embryos in a company laboratory in La Jolla, California, vehemently opposed reproductive (as opposed to therapeutic) cloning, insisting that it would be unethical as well as illegal.

among researchers and authorities alike that the old ethical objections had simply evaporated. The old case against human reproductive cloning had centered on issues specific to the human species, or to individual humans, but with the emphasis firmly on how they were a special case on account of their humanness as well as their individuality. But mongrels were not humans, and as that simple fact came to be widely and then near-universally accepted, the grounds for opposing research into mongrel reproductive cloning dropped away. Slyson and the other large producers began to pour vast amounts into just this sort of research, and within a very few years had started to achieve breakthroughs. There have now been a series of those, but they are inevitably lumped together when people speak of the reproductive revolution in chattel production. Within no more than a decade, everything reproductive for mongrels and chattels was turned on its head. An elaborate system of *maisons de préparation* was no longer required; many of the concerns about the outcomes of mongrel pregnancies among humans disappeared, as did all the worry over how the majority of the population was being excluded simply on economic grounds from enjoying the nutritional value and the extraordinary taste of yurn; prices started to fall, and kept falling.* You could produce chattel from chattel and accomplish relatively quickly and efficiently through science all the goals that society agreed needed to be striven for. Shorter lifecycles and harvest times, animals that could be perfectly bulked out in the weeks prior to harvesting, animals that could have removed from them the last vestiges of traits no longer needed in the species (most notably, speech and some of the other "higher" mental activities that a chattel had no need of)—all this could now be readily accomplished through the wonders of genetic engineering.†

---

*In my own view, perhaps the most important aspect of the change is that we are now able, should we as a society decide to do so, to address properly the issue of social inequality from the perspective of food supply. The revolution continues to have a powerful positive effect on price and availability; it is now possible not only for the rich and the moderately well-off but also for many working-class people to consume meat to an extent that has not been possible since the first half of the last century, in the final decades before the great extinctions.

†In recent years, of course, the problem has begun to be in the other direction. With the rate of mongrel births among humans still high, and chattel operations more and more productive, the problem of oversupply has become chronic. To some

Talk of the reproductive revolution goes somewhat beyond the focus of the story being told in these pages; that great upheaval in chattel farming was still on the horizon when the events of this narrative unfolded. But I do want you to be able to see it all in its various stages. And I want you to understand, in particular, that even *before* the reproductive breakthroughs, things had reached what seemed to all the experts to be a highly efficient equilibrium. The market ensured that incentives were always at roughly the right level to facilitate a steady supply of product (though inevitably, the very long lead times meant that occasional unanticipated surges of demand would lead to price spikes and shortages). The chattel farms became more and more sophisticated, with productivity reaching levels that could hardly have been imagined when the industry had been in its infancy. The average age for harvesting fell to under ten, as methods were developed to achieve even at this age body frames so well filled out as to produce over 90 pounds of pure yurn, with a further 35 to 55 pounds of processed yield. And the system was working efficiently in other ways too. Crucially, chattels spent less and less time in the unproductive nursery stage. With proper training, the new chattels were able to contribute as workers in the chattel industry's associated businesses by the age of three.*

---

extent this has been addressed by the introduction of new products; mongrels of marginal physical abilities that might once have nevertheless been worked for years in chattel farms are now marketed after only a few months as early yurn. It's not to my taste but I do see the logic of it, and many, of course, regard it as a delicacy, a truly unique flavor.

*Tasks were so structured that the combinations of muscle activity required could make a truly significant economic contribution to the adjunct businesses while never producing too much toughness or stringiness in the flesh of the final product. As was discovered, some extremely uncomfortable or exhausting tasks have no deleterious effects on the meat, while conversely, some tasks that place no particularly onerous burden on the chattel, and that may not even be associated with above-average levels of productivity, may nevertheless have severely negative effects on flesh and muscle quality when assessed from a consumer viewpoint. No correlations between discomfort or exhaustion and lower meat quality could be assumed, and indeed, it was important from the producer's point of view to resolutely ignore discomfort and exhaustion per se, and focus only on productivity and product quality. The trick for the chattel industry was to find the routines that resulted in the highest levels of productivity in the adjunct businesses with little or no negative impact on flesh quality. And of course the large operators became very, very good at it.

But I suspect I am asking you to understand much too much. Enough commentary—more than enough, no doubt. Back to the manuscript.

• •

L ike most families, the Stinsons talked about all this themselves sometimes. The subject of mongrels and chattels came up in conversation in any household at least once or twice a year. "What do you think about eating meat?" "What do you think about the chattel industry?" And so on. As in a lot of families, the one who voiced the doubts most forcefully was the youngest member of the family.

"Mommy, Daddy," Naomi burst out one day at the dinner table. This was just after she had turned ten. "I don't think we should serve chattel meat. Or goat meat.* I don't think we should eat any meat at all. Even birds, birds have brains too, they have feelings, I read to you about Alex from the book, remember?" The family was hardly likely to eat the flesh of a parrot,† but to the child it was somehow all one and the same. "We don't have to serve . . ."

"But it's *natural*, little Gnome. You're a lovely child and that's a lovely thought, but you can't ask people to do what doesn't come naturally to them."

"You can, Mommy, you can!" She angrily brushed away the tear that was starting to form at the far corner of her left eye. "You just don't care!"

---

*I will presume here that readers have at least a passing familiarity with the story of how, even though goats had miraculously escaped the great extinctions of the species, intensive farming of goats proved to be highly problematic, and goat meat has remained a small specialty-market item only.

†In her book *No Chance: The Disappearance of the Species*, Phyllis Tucker has famously argued that once the spread of antibiotic-resistant diseases had begun to gather steam it quickly became inevitable that the loss of species would not be restricted to birds and mammals that had been bred for consumption, or, indeed, to the species of pets that had in some cases lived in close proximity to them. Others have argued that at various points along the way a significant element of chance was involved. To my mind no fully adequate explanation has been provided as to why, for example, most parrots should have survived while budgerigars became extinct.

"I care for you, I care for us as a family, I care for people every-where. In that order. And further down the list—quite a bit further down the list, I'll admit—I care for animals. *Dumb animals*, they used to be called before we got all fussy with words, of course they can be loveable, but my guess is they got to be called *dumb animals* for a reason. Your Alex, even, what were they able to teach him, not even a hundred words. After years and years of trying he had fewer words than a toddler . . ."

"But Mommy, we don't eat toddlers."

"That's not the point, Naomi. A toddler will acquire these things, a toddler has the potential to grow into something with all the skills, logic, grammar, all that. And that's just one part of a larger whole. A toddler has the potential to be richly, fully human, to become a Shakespeare, a Georgia O'Keeffe, a Virginia Woolf. Birds and ani-mals are dumb, Naomi, you just can't get around it. I love the way you care about this, but you have to come to realize that human life is special, there's a sanctity to it—the bottom line is, a human life is worth more than a non-human one." Carrie paused, and out of her mouth at the pause's end came, "Here, have some more pasta. Your father's made it beautifully tonight." She passed the plate with some forcefulness, but it stayed where she set it down, halfway across the table.

"Well," put in Zayne, but he did not leave it at that, he paused and carried on. "I sort of think your mother's right about this one," he said carefully. "Though I don't think I can think through all the arguments as clearly as you can," he added, turning now to Carrie rather than to his daughter. "Maybe I'm counting on other things to make me just as richly human!" But his tone was falling flat, he could see that, he wanted to lighten things up a bit but the child seemed as unwavering as her mother. Why did Naomi have to take life so seriously? She was still so young, God knows every life had enough that was serious in it when the time came, enough and more. "No, I know none of this is a joke," he forestalled both of the others before they could say it. "All this about rationality, human potential, moral worth, all the rest of it—I'm just not sure I know what to make of it. And I *have* tried," he added hastily. "In fact there's been an awful lot of this on the news lately." Zayne said this as if it were somehow confirmation of his having tried to work through the complex issues, and at some level that is probably what he did believe. (If so, his perception was in two respects flawed; hearing a good deal of a four-part public-radio series on these issues had given him the sense that they were being much discussed in the popular media just then, when in fact that radio series had been very much an isolated case.)

"Mommy, Daddy, you can't! You can't really think it's all right to eat them." Naomi began to shake uncontrollably. Zayne went round the table to where she was sitting, held her, began to lift her in his arms. He did not know quite what to think about Sam. No, one did not want to eat such creatures, but perhaps one needn't feel too close to them either. It was hard to know what to think—or how to square what one thought with what Carrie might think. When it came to people, his daughter was the one he felt clearly and strongly about, perhaps the only one. And she needed him now; he was acutely aware that she needed him now.

"Come on, I'll take you upstairs and it *will* be all right, you'll see." At first she beat her small fists against his chest, but then she allowed herself to be carried up, to nuzzle Sam, to be settled with her daddy for a story. But his mind did not seem to be all on the story, there were other things he wanted to say. "I don't think I really agree *all* that much with what your mother was saying," he whispered to Naomi, patting down the covers as he spoke, "perhaps not so much, really. It's true that sometimes I don't know what to think, and then I don't honestly think I *can* think all of it through very well myself. Sort of like when you're trying to mix a green but then you can't help a bit of red smooshing in with the blue and the yellow, and you think that might make it more bright and clear after all but instead it gets more muddy and then you try adding a bit of a different blue and something else, but then suddenly it's all gone brown and it's just a muddle. This all feels a bit like that to me, a bit like a muddle. But I have to say I sometimes have a feeling like you do—that there's something wrong about it all.

"Anyway, it's not finished, what I was going to say down there. But sometimes you have to give in a little, you have to seem to be . . .

Maybe that's not it," he started again after a moment's pause. But this time the words trailed away.

"I love you Daddy. And I love Mommy," she added a little bit more quietly. "And I love Sam too!" This was the loudest, by quite a lot. She paused, and she thought about what she had been told in Sunday school. "I don't have to love Sam but I have to love you and Mommy."

"You don't have to feel anything, Naomi. You have to *do* certain things in life. Your mother knows more about that than I do, I guess. But you don't have to make your heart follow. Sometimes you can't, no one can." Then it was all right, and they finished the story and then he kissed her forehead, once, twice, three times, as he said the words "once, twice, three times," just as either he or her mommy had done at bedtime almost every night of her life, and then the rest of the words they always said, "all the night, and all the days, and over and over and over all the years."

"The thing I was thinking," Zayne began later, when he and Carrie were both settled in, reading in the living room, "the thing I was thinking when Naomi was getting so upset, one thing I started to think, anyway, is that if animals are less valuable than humans, than human life—and I grant that you're pretty persuasive on that—does that justify our treating them as badly as we might feel like doing, or as badly as it will take to make their meat as cheap as it can possibly be? Treat them that badly through the whole course of their lives? So far as I understand it, some of the things that go on in these factory farms really are unspeakable. But maybe we're not justified in eating them regardless, I guess that's another question. Maybe we shouldn't, even if we treated them well before killing them. When we *could* eat other things, things that have no senses, things that can't feel any pain."

"Yes, Zayne, those really are separate questions. Sometimes I think you're as much of a child as your daughter is." Those words might look harsh when they are set down on the page, but Carrie was relaxed and warm as she said them; she spoke almost lovingly, with wry humor. "You're no genius, Zayne, but you're a good man. I think we should stop all this brain talk and go to bed. And if you like . . ." She left that sentence unfinished. *And if you like . . .* was for them a well-worn code of the sort that exists in any marriage, even a marriage in which the partners don't feel that sort of warmth all that often, a marriage in which *go to bed* by itself almost always means simply what the words say—perhaps especially in that sort of marriage. Zayne ran his finger from the small of her back upward, and then down her spine again as the two went up the stairs. It was quiet now in Naomi's room, and they were careful to be quiet too in pressing the bedroom door closed, in muffling the sounds of the mattress and the springs as much as they could.

Anyone seeing Carrie and Zayne and Naomi walking Sam in the park or playing with him at the beach would sense that as a family they loved that sort of outing. Naomi, of course, was endlessly devoted. And Carrie and Zayne could not help but bask in the joy she radiated. Of course Zayne could never warm to Sam in the way that—well, a mongrel could never be the son he had never . . . Such thoughts would always trail off; there was no need to dwell on any of that. But at the appropriate distance Zayne was always friendly to Sam. Sometimes he would even fondle his tousled hair, albeit in an oddly distracted fashion. And even Carrie was often friendly to the creature. There was almost never any physical contact between her and Sam, but she did express a degree of warmth toward him; it was hard not to, for she loved her daughter and all this was clearly bringing Naomi so much happiness.

They always dressed him in a smart, clean coverall,* usually a cheery yellow or green. Over time the one-piece coverall had estab-

---

*[Broderick Clark's note] The matter of how best to clothe a mongrel was one that periodically received a fair amount of attention in home lifestyle magazines and daytime talk shows on radio and the seescreen. Everyone agreed you couldn't dress a mongrel like a human, and everyone agreed you couldn't dress it like a chattel in a finishing pen either, which is to say, to keep it mostly or entirely unclothed.

lished itself as the norm for pet mongrels, but that still left a lot of room for variation and for fashion. Others might allow their mongrel to go gallivanting about in a dirty old gray coverall, but not the Stinsons. If there was one thing they were firm about, Zayne even more than Carrie, it was that. And they rarely used a leash unless propriety demanded it. They weren't the sort of family to always be pulling a creature this way and that, bossing it around. They would always treat their mongrel kindly and humanely.

And so they did for many, many months, all of them. But after the first year or so you might notice if you paid close attention that fewer and fewer of the smiles and the laughs when the family was out together on this sort of occasion came from Carrie. When Carrie smiled at Sam it became a half smile, or even something less. She liked to see her daughter happy, and she was prepared to go to some lengths to ensure that she stayed that way; she loved Naomi more than anything or anyone. She would also go some distance toward making sure that Zayne stayed happy, happy enough at any rate. To have an unhappy household, a divided household, was an enormous drain on everyone's time and energy, more of a drain than a lot of people realized when they started getting divorced willy-nilly, Carrie was sure of that. It was worth expending a lot of real effort to avoid any of that happening. But there were things about the whole situation with Naomi and Sam that she didn't like, that she didn't feel comfortable with, there was no sense pretending otherwise. Naomi was happy, she had to think Naomi was happy in some sense of the word, but it was not a normal sort of happiness, not a normal sort of happiness for a child of her age. Naomi was almost a tween now, life for her should more and more be revolving around her friends, but outside of school she seemed to have less and less desire to spend time with other children. It was always walks with Sam, Sam this and Sam that. If she got together with other girls her own age it was almost always something her parents had set up, not something she had initiated, she would never say *Mommy, Daddy, can Sarah come over after school?* Or, *Mommy, Daddy, can I go for a sleepover with Jenny and Elizabeth on Saturday?* Was that healthy for a child, not to have any of that side of life? Carrie couldn't imagine that it could be healthy. Would the child just grow out of it? How could you be sure? Could you allow that sort of a situation to go on indefinitely? Zayne didn't seem to think there was anything to worry about, but that was Zayne. When did he ever think there was anything to worry about?

Carrie had nothing against Sam, really, nothing at all. He had that crudeness of appearance that all mongrels had—but she had to admit he had those things in a good deal less abundance than did many of them; physically he could hardly be called attractive, but nor was he repulsive in the way that some them were. And he certainly had a pleasant temperament; on balance, as Carrie would sometimes acknowledge to herself, almost in surprise, she genuinely liked him. But as to what was really going on between the creature and Naomi—how was one to know? Goodness knows she spent enough time making sure that he was well behaved. The clarity and forcefulness with which Carrie had laid things out at the beginning had paid off, that much was certain. And despite what Carrie had said initially, issues of cost were not a serious concern, any more than were issues of convenience. Even the most expensive brands of mongrel food did not make a significant dent in the household budget of someone at the level Carrie was at. And if they went away on holiday and wanted to leave Sam behind, finding a teenager to stop in to top off the feed and make sure everything was okay was not difficult. No, it was nothing having to do with the logistics that bothered her. Maybe she should be like Zayne, just put it out of her mind. After all, there was nothing she could put her finger on, nothing specific. But sometimes when Carrie would see Naomi and Sam playing in the sun she would think, *It's not crazy to worry, it really isn't. She should be spending time with girls her own age, I know she should.* And then she would think again, *Maybe the feeling is just nothing, really, maybe it will just go away with time, Naomi will change with time, of course she will.* But then the other sort of feeling would come back. She would have liked to have made more of a fuss about it, been more direct about it with Zayne, been prepared to argue it through. That was the way she always believed in doing things, after all. But this was different, what could you say that had any substance, really? And could she really trust her own feelings over this sort of a situation? No, she didn't really think she could; again, this sort of thing really was different. She knew when she was honest with herself that there was a real chance in this case her judgment could be clouded, that whatever doubts she had about Sam and about all the attention Naomi paid to Sam might not stem from what was happening between the two of them now. There was a feeling she had about Sam that was part of a larger feeling she had about all mongrels and chattels. It was not a feeling she wanted to talk about, not with Zayne, not with anyone, but she knew the feeling was in her, and in her to stay. And she knew it was capable of shaping her thoughts about Naomi and Sam.

Sometimes, half awake in the early hours, in a haze of half memory, half light, and half fear, it would come back to her and she would try not to remember the horror from that last term at university. In those days the first really large chattel farms were just starting to be set up. That spring she drove by the vast farm at Brooks that even then covered hundreds of acres. That year they were replacing the wire mesh they had originally put in for fencing, replacing it with the opaque, ten-foot-high electrified variety that has now long been established as the industry standard. As she was passing by the work was still unfinished, and you could see everything, acre after acre of dirty little chattels grubbing in the fields, and in the near pens chattels in the final stages before harvesting, hundreds of them in the foul smelling, muddy enclosure, crammed in so they wouldn't move around too much during the final fattening. The deep repulsion she had felt had never left her. For months she had to force herself not to think, as she ate a lettuce and tomato salad or a bowl of fruit, of the filthy creatures who had picked the stuff in fields like the ones she had seen. Picked it, and handled it, handled all of it with their grimy little hands.

That had been the second year she had been going out with Dieter—later to become a VP at Barwell Engineering. Back then he was just a young man who had lost his way taking English and history, a man who had not yet discovered he could find fulfillment as an engineer, a young man who was taking out his frustrations on everyone around him. As Carrie and Dieter's relationship started to drag on, it began to feel almost like an act of violence when they made love, though each time he would stroke her afterward, and tell her how much she excited him. Sometimes he would say it gently, almost as if *you excite me* were the same as *I love you*, other times he would say it more forcefully, almost accusingly, as if whatever brutality he had just given vent to had its source in her rather than in him.

She was always very careful, but one Monday that spring she felt nauseated and somehow she knew that, despite all her precautions, something was growing inside her. With that thought came another in a rush, a thought uncontrollable, frightful, unstoppable. An animal was growing inside her, a dirty and disgusting little vegetable-faced animal, an animal with something of the look of a human in its limbs and its torso but a thing debased, a creature of no mental powers, ruled by crude instincts and raw appetites. She saw the continuum among all these creatures of minimal mental powers: fetuses, chattels, the cows and pigs that had been a part of her parents' world. And she wanted no part of it, especially not with anything that issued from her as a result of what Dieter had done to her, what he kept wanting to do to her night after night after night after night.

She split up with him the next Saturday ("I can see it's going to be better for you to have your freedom" were the words she used, and she kept her composure throughout the difficult little discussion), for she wanted him neither to know what had happened inside her nor to be in any way a part of her life when she had the thing removed.

The procedure had been carried out within the month, and a calm came down like a soft curtain over a part of Carrie's mind. There would be no need for her to deal with animals again. She had chosen Zayne without animal ardor herself, and in full awareness that he was not, even in those days when he was young, a person dominated by animal passion in the way that many young men are. She found means of ensuring a degree of responsiveness on those occasions when responsiveness was appropriate, but such occasions—somewhat infrequent even in the early years of their relationship—became increasingly rare as the years went on. When Carrie became pregnant with Naomi she did not allow herself to imagine for a moment that within her might be an animal thing and not a human one. When the ultrasound and the other tests seemed to suggest that it was likely to be fully human, she allowed a tight smile to cross her face and allowed Zayne to embrace her in a gesture that she trusted would make plain both to him and to the nurses that this was precisely what she had expected, that there was no need for guarded relief or cautious celebration of the sort that many couples gave voice to at these moments; she wished to project a sense of serene certainty that only something fully human could grow inside her.

When she would lie in that half light between sleep and waking years later, she sometimes more than half understood that her attitude toward Sam could have been shaped by those earlier times more than she would like to think. What she felt—was it a legitimate worry about her daughter's welfare? Or was it some weird aversion to little Naomi spending all her time with something sub-human? She would look at that squat, stocky little figure and that large, sloping forehead and she would have to admit to herself that she didn't know, she just didn't know. So instead of coming right out and saying to Zayne how worried she was about Naomi, how she didn't think their daughter should be focused so much on her pet, she should be more like other little girls, Carrie would procrastinate. Again and again she would think of saying something, again and again she would stop herself.

We are never able to hide things from our children as well as we think we are able to hide them; children know so much of what we try to shield them from. And Naomi knew perfectly well that something in her mommy felt a sort of revulsion toward Sam, she even knew the word, *revulsion*, she read a lot of books now with words like that in them. And so she knew that her mommy could never love Sam as she loved Sam. Or maybe even as her daddy loved Sam, as Naomi thought he did, anyway, Daddy never lied about his feelings but sometimes they would come and go or sort of wobble a little, like Jell-O, and Mommy's feelings were not like that. It was Mommy she had to worry about. Mommy couldn't be allowed to know, that was the thing above all. If she discovered that they had a pet mongrel who was learning words just like any human, Naomi felt sure she would see it not as something wondrous, but as something freakish. And maybe other people would see it that way too, Naomi could not guess. But she knew she did not want Mommy to know about her and Sam and what he could do, she did not want that sort of knowing, she wanted only to think of the knowing that was happening with Sam and with her. From *baa* and *caa* she had been able to move on not just to *car* and *far* but to *care* and *fair*. And *un* had led to *bun* and *run* and *sun* and *fun*, and on and on to *ee* and *ay* and *see* and *key* and *me* and *bye* and *high* and *why*. It had all opened up. Sam could not make the sounds in the same way that Naomi could, but he *could* make them in his own way. And every day he learned more of them, learned more ways to put them together, the whole world was opening.

Sometimes he could hardly stop smiling, something rushed through his heart as everything was rushing through his head. He could put together all the words every which way, the thinks that were so bright and new, and he felt a knowing that now he would always be loving Naomi, not maybe in the same way as he had loved his mother, but as strongly, just as strongly. That was something he knew was not for putting into words but something to hold inside himself.

They worked at it together, always ever so quietly so Carrie would not find out. Every day, month after month, up in the attic usually, not anywhere where Carrie might hear, might discover what was going on. But Naomi couldn't ask him to whisper. Even when he spoke quietly it was often hard to make out what he meant—so hard that she had to strain and struggle and stroke his arms while she said, speaking ever so slowly herself, "one . . . more . . . time. Slow-ly. One . . . more . . . time," and he would try again and again to arrange his lips just so, to push the air out in a way that looked as it did when she did it. He often wished that he could see the air itself, not just how she moved her lips and her tongue around it. But for all their frustrations, it kept happening quickly: words, phrases, whole sentences, thoughts that were bigger than things put into words. And stories too. Not just the stories in Naomi's books, but Sam's story too, the story of what it had been like for him at the old house, with Tammy and Broderick and Daniel and Letitia. It was hard for him to speak of that, not just hard to find the words and make them, but hard in the other way. It was better when they talked about other things, about how the sun could shine on the moon, or on China. And bowls that were china, and where the river that went through the town came from, how it went through the United States and then Canada, and then the United States again, how it started in the mountains and meandered through the plains and through the badlands, and what it was like when it passed by them, and how you could follow it into the bigger river with the lovely name, the Missouri, and the bigger river still with the other lovely name but that was a little bit funny too, Mississippi. And what had happened when all the land between the city at the end of the Mississippi and the place where they were themselves, all that land in between and out to the sides too had been bought from France, that was the sort of thing Sam liked to find out about.

Like Sam, Naomi didn't want to talk about certain sorts of feelings. But there was a special warmth that they shared somehow. And Naomi knew that was another thing that Carrie couldn't be allowed to know, another reason why she mustn't find out even about the talking, how Sammy was almost like a human, really, it was only how he pronounced things. But they couldn't always stay in Naomi's room, or in the attic. Sometimes they would sit together in the garden, in a little space behind a hedge at the back, that was good because anyone glancing through the window at the back of the house would not see that they were there. And twice a day, of course, they would go on their walks.* The walks were wonderful for them both. For Sam it could be like an Expotition, tracking the Woozles with Pooh Bear or an Expotition with Christopher Robin to a thing that you discover and you could bring Provisions, and for Naomi it could be like that too; she could pretend to be littler again. She would also think of the

---

*[Broderick Clark's note] This habit—one of the many holdovers from the days of domestic dogs that you find in the conventions that grew up to address the proper treatment of the new pets—became the norm with all pet mongrels early on; it was expected that they would be walked twice a day.

things you had to think of when you were responsible for someone else, of course, but that was always a burden she carried with a smile, and a tiny bit of pride too. And she could always feel relaxed; when she and Sam were out together Naomi did not have to worry about Carrie becoming suspicious. Nothing could be more natural than for a child to take the family's pet mongrel around a few blocks and through the park and along the path by the river twice a day, even if it was cold or it was raining, everyone knew that was what you had to do. Especially along the river, where she knew one path that was overgrown, not like the main path, the paved path on the other side, but a path sometimes half hidden by juniper and wild roses that you had to push through, a path where they could just be themselves, together.

That's not to say that Naomi didn't sometimes think of Sam as different. It wasn't always easy to think of him as human, as entirely human, not when he sounded as he did. But none of that mattered— not really, not except for that one day, maybe three years after Sam had come to them. They had been coming back along the river on the other side, along the paved path. It had been a strange walk, strange and a little frightening; a thunderstorm had broken just as they had come to the place with the fast water where the parkland widens and there are a lot of picnic tables and fire pits. They had found shelter under a raised platform in the little playground there, and they had stayed dry while the rain poured down around them. The lightning had been so close and the thunder so loud, they were safe in their little refuge except it was frightening when the thunder was so sudden and so very loud. But Naomi noticed something in Sam: he didn't get frightened, not really, even when the thunder cracked right on top of them, he never flinched, never whimpered, it was as if he didn't hear a thing. But the storm passed quickly and as they came out into the open, rays of sun were already glinting off the swings and the slides. Others had come out from shelter too, a large group, it seemed like three or four families, they all seemed to know each other. They had all been cooking on the fire pits, they had protected them with the iron covers while it was raining but now the covers were off and you could see that meat was on the grill, a lot of meat and the smell was very strong, so strong that Naomi wrinkled her nose and made a face, and Sam asked what it was, and then she told him all about what the smell was, what they were cooking and all about where it came from. And that made Sam's face go all funny. He had never understood what yurn was, he knew it was something that people had sometimes at home, but they didn't feed him any and he didn't know why. Now he couldn't get away from the thoughts, and from the nightmares. Not just that night but nightmares that kept coming back, she had told him that the smell was from the flesh, and she had told him where they sent them, and how they lived, the little that she knew of it, of what happened in the Repositories and at the chattel farms, and what happened to them at the end before they were packaged in pieces for the supermarket shelves. She did not think as she spoke of what Sam was, she just let out all the words about how she felt, and about how wrong it was, and of course he would feel that it was wrong too. But it was a different feeling for him, of course it would be a different feeling for him, she should have thought of that, she saw that now. But now was too late and she had upset him, and she was very, very sorry.

Broderick, many years later

I HAVE ALREADY touched on some of the ways in which chattel farming, profitable though it could be, could also be a daunting proposition, especially before it became an established, proven moneymaker. It wasn't only the legal issues that required resolution; it was also how to deal with the element of time—the long gestation period to start with, and then there was a vast time issue after that as well. It was one thing to harvest mongrels in infancy—and that was done often enough in the early days, whatever was surplus at the Repository would be harvested, regardless of age. But to establish a chattel farm and run it as a proper business you had to have a product with enough flesh to make the whole operation viable. In practice, as came to be agreed after a period of experimentation, you needed at least sixty to seventy pounds of usable product from each carcass. Excuse me for using this blunt language, but that was of course how one had to think if one was to make a business of it. You needed that much usable product, and at first the highest ratio of usable product to full body weight was two to three; in other words, you needed animals weighing in at close to a hundred pounds before you could make any projections for a truly profitable business on a sustainable basis, a reliable basis. To start with, you had to invest in raising the creatures through infancy—though the investment there could be capped by using older chattels as workers in the chattel nurseries; it wasn't as if you needed to hire a full complement of human laborers. But you couldn't economically harvest them at the end of infancy and be more than marginally profitable; you couldn't achieve the right ratios. In the first days of chattel farming it was thought that the earliest you would be able to economically harvest a chattel, getting good ratios and a really decent profit margin, would be after twelve or thirteen years, no matter what penning and feeding methods you adopted. Even the gains in efficiency of the early years of the industry brought that number down only to ten or eleven. You just couldn't get a chattel to bulk up properly at an earlier age than that, and the flesh would be so poorly marbled that it would often fetch less than half the Chicago Mercantile price for grade A. That meant you had to commit to at least ten years of upkeep, ten years of feed. And waiting ten years for a chattel to mature wasn't like waiting ten years for a vineyard to grow in properly; you had to feed it more than water and sunlight. Even if you accepted that yurn would be a luxury product, not something for the masses, how many people could you expect would pay and keep paying the sort of prices that an almost-ten-year development process would have necessitated? Chattel operations would have had to charge almost unbelievably extravagant prices on an ongoing basis had there not been some change in another part of the equation.

There was, of course, just such a breakthrough.* The great innovation was simply to realize the labor potential of chattel prior to harvesting. In a very real sense this was not a new idea. In the seventeenth or eighteenth century a team of oxen would become food once their working days were over. The same could be said, indeed, of a good deal of the food chain in the nineteenth century and even into the twentieth. Oxen, dairy cattle, plough horses, draw horses—all would inevitably end up as food, and people were not too fussy about the degree of toughness all those working years might have imparted to the meat. A lot of it would end up ground or stewed, in any case, and back then people were used to marinating meat to make it tender.

So it wasn't an entirely new idea, but sometimes reviving an old idea

---

*An important bit of background to the story here is often left out. When people recount the development of the "product-pays-its-way" business model they often neglect to mention the part played by government subsidies. The large companies considering expansion into the chattel business were from the start pretty sure of being able to tap into government coffers; after all, the immensely profitable beef and chicken and pork producers of the old days had consistently been able to persuade governments to give them incentives in virtually every Western country. Wouldn't the nascent chattel-farming industry, with the huge costs and huge risks associated with its unique investment time line, be at least as worthy a candidate for government incentives as the old meat producers? Sure enough, when the fear of nutritional deficiency began to spread through the population, government "stepped up to the plate" for meat producers to an unprecedented degree.

can seem as fresh as thinking up a brand-new one. And it had been such a very long time since the practice of turning work animals into feed at the end of their productive lives had gone out of fashion.

Critics suggested that here again there should be a legal issue—that acquiring labor in this way should fall under the statutes that set minimum wages and regulated working conditions. It would have done so, of course, had the legal cases over the larger issue of the status of mongrels and chattels gone the other way. Once it had been established that a chattel was not a human person, however, it proved impossible to claim on any legal grounds that it should be paid as a person. That a chattel would be harvested after a set number of productive years did not in essence make it any different from a machine that might do the same work over the same period and be sold at the end of it.

At first a number of producers tried to find secondary businesses that wouldn't require a lot of capital outlay but that had the potential to bring in large and steady returns. Warehousing was a favorite: depending on the type of goods involved and on how quick the turnover, it was a business that could be highly labor-intensive, and if your labor costs were effectively zero—if chattels who would otherwise be idling about in their pens could do the work—that gave you a huge advantage over your competitors. The older ones could lug paint cans off the shelves and (with a bit of training) shift heavy skids with forklifts, the smaller ones could put together retail orders for hinges, thumbtacks, toggle nuts, or toothpaste tubes, anything smaller than they were, in other words. It all sounded ideal, but there turned out to be a good many problems with the concept. The chattels needed a lot of direction, so in fact you could never reduce your labor costs to zero, not even close. And even with the clearest and firmest instructions, you could count on them making many, many mistakes. It's easy to understand the potential for damage from mistakes in operations dealing with a lot of small items: the youngest useable chattels were nimble, but could perform only to the absolute lowest levels mentally, meaning supervisors had to check and double-check to prevent selection and shipping errors. But even in operations that used older chattels and that involved fewer product items, there turned out to be significant problems. When Slyson Foods bought out Consolidated Paint, they found that in their Greeley operation alone they were averaging three major incidents daily—a "major incident" being defined as one causing significant loss of operational time, or product, or both. If a chattel miscalculated in accessing a skid of large drums of latex base from the highest storage level, that could mean the loss of thousands of dollars in top-quality product and several hours of clean-up downtime. And the clean-up would often have to involve the chattel itself. If a limb had been broken or crushed in the incident or if there had been other damage, it would need to be sedated, penned, tagged, and set aside for transport to the meatpacking plant. Simple enough in itself, but the fact was that such incidents typically had a ripple effect with the other chattels; they would become nervous and distracted, all of which was in turn likely to lead to further incidents, further work stoppages. Slyson was astounded and dismayed to find that even after the new managers at Consolidated had had three years to "work out the kinks" of using a chattel workforce, they were still not quite able to match the productivity ratios of Color Coat. The market leader had taken a precisely opposite tack, investing what had been for them unprecedented amounts of capital in new machinery and new software. For virtually every warehouse task Color Coat was now using computerized machinery rather than either chattels or a human labor force. A lot of analysts had called them crazy when they announced their strategy to meet the Slyson/Consolidated challenge, but three years later the naysayers had disappeared. The Color Coat approach had worked, and the Slyson strategy of using chattels for warehouse labor was as thoroughly discredited as had been the notion back in the 1930s and 1940s that horse-drawn delivery could compete against gasoline or diesel.

In the end, most producers turned to what many early on had said was the obvious secondary operation—mixed farming. A chattel didn't need a lot of mental acuity to pick an orange or to tend a tomato plant or to harvest a head of lettuce. So long as it had functioning limbs and digits it would be perfectly up to the task. To make it truly cost-effective you had to have work for the available chattels all the time, and that meant a large operation with a lot of different crops. But as time went on a lot of companies began to demonstrate that it was very doable. More than a few other companies were furious; if a company had been doing everything it could to cut costs producing lettuce and tomatoes with low-wage and usually illegal immigrant labor, it was galling to see others come along and exploit legal loopholes to undercut its position, arranging things so as to have the work done essentially for free. But there was little the old-style conventional producers could do to vent their envy and anger—other than make the transition to chattel farming themselves.*

I should make plain (for any that are not aware of it) that not all farms have been run the same way, that not all chattels have been treated in the same fashion. Here and there small farms years ago began to adopt a very different approach: a "free-range" or "pure organic" approach to the raising of chattels. (I suppose here I should declare something of a conflict of interest. As most of you know, I have for years been associated with an organization that promotes just this sort of approach. I will have something more to say about this alternative in a moment—and I have written a good deal about it elsewhere.) But in an intensive operation,

---

*To be sure, there remained some who argued that from a business perspective combining chattel farming with other forms of farming was not an optimal approach. Their line of reasoning was that, much as such an approach might show at first a powerful flow-through to the bottom line as a result of reduction in labor costs, in the long term the cost of labor was *too* low; it acted as an inappropriately powerful disincentive to invest in capital improvements. If chattels were available to pick your lettuce or your oranges for free, you were not likely to consider investing in picking and sorting machines that might in the long run be more reliable and more efficient.

My own view, for what it's worth, is that these supposedly business-minded critics had not themselves thought through everything in the round, with a view to the long term. Above all, they failed to appreciate that not everyone wants a factory-farmed product. If you want a truly high-end product, in terms of taste and consumer health, then you want organic. You want no pesticides, you want no herbicides, you want no fungicides. And certainly now, with prices having dropped so dramatically in the wake of the reproductive revolution, price should be less of an issue—great taste and the healthiest product will more and more be what people want. But you'll never be able to get such a product except through a highly labor-intensive operation. And that's what a secondary chattel operation can give you—labor-intensive, but unbeatable costs.

My own concern regarding chattel farming, then, is not at all with the fundamentals of combining chattel farming with other forms of farming as a secondary business; it is with the degree to which the large companies have allowed their operations to be run on an inhumane basis. If anything, the companies should raise prices. That way consumers could be reassured that they were buying a high-end product offering not only great taste and environmentally friendly means of production, but also humane treatment throughout.

when the animals reach the final finishing stage and are no longer put to use in the fields, they are typically allowed no more than two and a half square yards apiece when the pens are full, and perhaps three to four times that when the operation has not yet reached its seasonal peak. To go above those numbers, according to the conventional wisdom, was simply uneconomic. If the chattels were free to roam about over a larger area during the final finishing stage, too much of the nourishment that had been put into them would go toward fueling physical activity, too little toward the product itself.

As the "alternative" farmers kept pointing out, there were serious disadvantages to intensive systems. People might disagree about whether the system could be reformed in such a way as to be consistent with the humane treatment of chattels, or whether the only way to achieve such a goal was to use entirely different methods. But there could be no doubt in the mind of anyone with a conscience who looked at the way things were run in the intensive operations as to the evils that they perpetrated. The close quarters in which the animals lived inevitably meant that when they would muck about in the feedlots, the muck would be composed of a good deal of their own excrement mixed in with the dirt or sand. And when not in the open lot, the animals would of course foul their own pens. Technology had been able to improve things somewhat. All except the most mentally deficient or rebellious animals would be able to relieve themselves over the grates, and the excrement would be carried via an elaborate system of tubes and channels into the covered lagoon that any operation was required to maintain. (The only exceptions to this were certain of the earliest intensive operations, which had been protected by a grandfather clause in the first legislation.) Even the most modern operations, though, were susceptible to outbreaks, and with so many animals in close proximity—the largest operations would have eight or nine thousand in their pens at one time—there was always a danger of infection spreading rapidly through the herd. The new drugs were extraordinarily effective; each animal received with its feed a daily low-level dose of antibiotics intended as preventative medicine, and a hyperantibiotic "cocktail" at the first sign of any significant infection of any member of the herd. But every operation had to live with the constant awareness of what had happened to producers back in the time of the great extinctions, as bacteria had developed with extraordinary rapidity resistance to antibiotics, with the result that not one industry but half a dozen related ones were wiped out inside of a generation.* There

_____

*That the same might happen again was the scenario the free-range advocates kept emphasizing—and for a time groups such as the one I am now associated with were taken very seriously by some influential voices in the media. They argued (I will say "they" rather than "we," for this was of course long before I was associated with the movement) that you didn't need to raise chattels through intensive farming, and that for all sorts of reasons you shouldn't do so. Their tone was more strident than that of our group and other similar ones today (most of them refused to ever use the term *intensive farming*, referring instead to *factory farming*). And that was a shame since most of what they had to say made complete sense. What they wanted were ranches and farms that ran on largely (if not entirely) free-range principles. There could be fences, sure, but most of the time chattels would be allowed to roam at will over common ground, with as few as eight hundred animals per acre. That such spaciousness would be beneficial to the animals could hardly be doubted; perhaps just as important, by keeping them from tramping around in their own feces, you would keep down the threat of disease, and the need for antibiotics. In the best operations—certified as organic—antibiotics were kept entirely out of the food chain, as were other non-naturally occurring chemicals. The free-range operations run on these principles did include pens, but chattels were given as much as twelve square yards apiece in the enclosed areas, and each pen had a concrete enclosed excreting area where the animals could press a button to have themselves hosed down, and have any residual excrement washed away through the grate. Free-range proponents readily conceded then (as we do today) that one effect of not confining the animals to a tightly restricted area through their entire lives is to make the meat tougher—*firmer* is perhaps a better word—and tangier. But more important, they argued from the beginning that it was far healthier. Numerous studies since have corroborated that claim, showing what switching to free-range kept emphasizing—meat can improve the condition of your heart, your waistline, even your liver and kidneys.

There has also been, of course, another group of activists, smaller but more vocal, who have been almost as dismissive of the organic and free-range producers as they have been of the factory farms—in some cases even more so. To my mind, many of these more extreme activists have been as unthinking as they have been shrill. For one thing, they have always failed to understand that chattels would not even have the benefit of existence in most cases if it were not for chattel farming. For another, they don't give enough credit to the free-range producers for adopting a humane approach and for providing to the chattels an existence that is not only pain-free up to the moment of harvesting, but even in most cases decidedly enjoyable. What good is it, they argue, giving the animals more space and more comfort if you are just going to kill them and eat them in the end anyway? They insist too that just eating meat—any meat—is bad for you, bad for your health as well as bad in terms of right and wrong. That a lot of the evidence they produce

had been literally tens of thousands of bankruptcies, and ripple effects had spread throughout the world economy. No matter how good the new hyper-pharmaceuticals were, there was always the chance that the scientists, the veterinarians, the drug companies would once again be proven wrong, that the same thing would happen once again.

• •

O*r-anj is bee-you-ti-full.*

Orange *was* beautiful. Her daddy didn't think so though, when they talked about the colors he used and Naomi made suggestions he would never put any orange into a painting, not one bit, he needed more bright sometimes and he didn't know it, that's what his daughter was beginning to think as she matured. And she was maturing, her parents didn't always see that but she was. But none of that had anything to do with why she was saying those words now, watching her own lips in the mirror. It was the mirror she had in the bedroom, and she had the door closed. She would always close the door whenever she was doing this, she didn't want anyone to see. Anyone except Sam, of course, it didn't matter if he was there, and in fact he was there with her now. Sometimes she liked to practice, to watch herself speaking, just to see how her mouth moved, to see that she was moving it right so the sounds would be all clear. She had started doing it months ago, with very simple sounds; now she did it with more complicated ones like the *bee-you* in *beautiful*, those were the sounds that Sammy seemed still to have a little trouble with. She wanted so much for all the sounds to be clear for him so he could hear just right. She could see how when he listened he looked at her mouth too, looked so intently, maybe that helped him to hear.

Then it came to her, all in a flash. Everything she had thought

---

in support of these assertions is highly dubious, I have no doubt. But I don't want to become intemperate in criticizing the vegetarian fringe, any more than I want to allow myself to be carried away in criticizing the excesses and outright cruelties that developed in the chattel industry as it adopted intensive practices.

about what little Sam did, everything she had thought about what he thought and how he thought—it was all just a little bit wrong, like something that has been twisted one notch away from where it should slide in. Sam had not been able to speak because he had not been able to hear. That was all there was to it, Naomi saw it now. The thunder that he had not flinched from, the time when she had had to pull him back from the train tracks to prevent him from walking right into the path of the engine even though it was sounding its horn full blast, the time that—there had been so many times, why hadn't she seen it earlier?

The realization washed over her now like a huge wave, pulling her mind one way, and then another way even more strongly with the undertow. Sam had been just behind her, sitting on the floor, his knees pulled up, a picture book resting on them. He looked up and immediately saw her face shattered into shards. Shock? Anguish? Joy? He could not tell, it was something that looked like joy, but she looked somehow pained too. He made his words: "Ill elp ou, let me elp ou!" Tears had started to come into her eyes but it was not so completely sad, he could see that, and then she hugged him, it was different from all the other hugs or almost all of them, it was stronger, and then she started to try to tell him why, she said to him slowly, her mouth right in front of his eyes, "You are not the sort of mongrel I thought you were at all, are you? That's why you have been able to talk like this, have been able to do everything, have been able to learn so quickly. You are as smart as I am—or as smart as I was when I was your age." Then she took him by the shoulders and looked into his eyes and held him by the ears. "These don't work, do they?" she said, very slowly and clearly, tugging gently on the lobes. "Your . . . ears . . . don't work! You are only able to talk because you watch my lips very closely, that's how you sort of hear, isn't it? You . . . watch . . . my lips . . . don't you?" Sam nodded and nodded, all the while with her hands tugging at his earlobes.

He was not sure what everything she had said meant, but it was as true as could be that he watched her lips.

"Es, es, ah do that. Evreone muz do that."

"But they *don't*, Sam, they don't, there are sounds that you can't see, there are . . ." She couldn't explain it all now, not while so much was rushing in her brain. She was glowing inside and out, radiant. It was not as it had been, everything was entirely new now, she could tell Mommy everything now, Mommy could not be shocked or horrified or fearful, there was nothing freakish about Sam now, if you were deaf you didn't have to be a mongrel. You could be accepted as human, when you were deaf that's usually what happened, that's always what happened if it was clear that you could learn to communicate. He could be a lovable human, deaf but lovable. And *human*. One of *them*—Naomi somehow knew how much that mattered to her mother, maybe to her father too. She suddenly saw everything, how it would all be different, how it would all work out. She started telling him how it would all work out, how it was so wonderful that he wasn't what he had seemed to be, how this solved everything, how everything would be so wonderful now.

Sam had lost the thread. Wasn't he what he had seemed to be? What was so wonderful? Hadn't it been all right with Naomi and him, with all of them? Naomi was going too fast for him, and he suddenly felt a little anxious. Her smile grew and grew, and just stayed there, until it somehow made Sam feel unlucky, as if something bad was about to happen. Nothing could be this happy. But he could not show her how worried it made him feel, not when she was so happy; he had never seen her so happy. And he managed it, she looked at him and there was enough reflected there that she could imagine him to be happy too. "I think we have to tell them right away, tell Mommy, that is, Daddy's not here today, I have to tell Mommy but you have to talk too and tell her that you have to look at people's lips to know what they are saying. And then she will see, she will see and everything will be all right and you can be my brother forever and ever. Little boys lead lives just as long as little girls, you know, they get to be old people, seventy or eighty years old, even older, not like how mongrels die so young, almost all of them do. I thought you were going to die on me before I was even grown up, and now I know you are going to live so long, so very long it's like forever. Come, come with me, we have to tell her!"

There was so much to make Naomi joyful—her special one would live a long time, maybe as long as she would, maybe longer; and now her mother wouldn't mind if they kept Sam forever, wouldn't mind, couldn't mind, they could bring him right into the family.

Naomi never thought for a moment of how the stigma of being a mongrel would now be gone; none of her joy came from that. She just didn't think in that sort of way; she had grown so used to thinking of mongrels as fellow creatures, no matter what was wrong with them, no matter if they could talk or not, no matter how long they might live. As different creatures, for sure, maybe as less capable ones. But all the same, creatures that it was important to care for and to keep from harm. That was how you should treat all creatures, it wasn't so complicated, really.

But Naomi had not thought everything through. If she had been a little older she might have thought twice, might have thought maybe there could be reasons *not* to tell everything to her mother. But she skipped away, pausing for Sam to join her as she went through the door, and pausing again at the top of the stairs to let Sam catch up. She was unable to contain herself, she was bursting with a happiness as big as any happiness there could be in the whole big world.

"I don't care *what* noises he can make. It might even sound a bit like speech. And maybe there even are a few actual words here and there. Some of them can manage that even when no one has been trying to teach them to parrot the sounds we make. But he's not what you think, Naomi, really he isn't. *Look* at him, Gnome. Look at his forehead, look at his features. It's not for no reason he's in coveralls!"

How could Carrie have let things get this far with her daughter? She had herself to blame more than the girl, that was what she told herself, right at the start she should have . . . Well, at least she could do something now, she would have to do something. Even Zayne would have to realize it had gone too far. "It's a crazy delusion, Gnome, it's all in your head. You've been spending too much time on your own, I'm afraid, too much time spinning fantasies about a mongrel. I'm sorry to have to put it like that, but that's the truth of it. When people start to go like that they . . . , well, the mind plays tricks. And they're not fun little tricks like little Saffron who used to be your friend does when she's been studying her magic books or she's bought something new from the novelty store. They can be nasty tricks, Naomi, very nasty tricks. You know what happens when people start to spin ideas like that?"

Carrie hated herself when she got like this, but somehow she couldn't stop herself. Her face was slowly getting redder and redder, too hot to get close to, like a burner with the electric current flowing through it and the resistance to the current keeps making it brighter and hotter, hotter and brighter. "It makes everything unsteady, *everything.* If you start saying things like that, thinking things like that, pretty soon people will be saying there's no line to be drawn. They'll start saying that anything which can move and can make noises is just like a human, is just as good as a human, should have everything a human has. But do you think a thing like that can take on the responsibilities of a human? *Do* you?" Her voice was alive with intensity, but somehow it still kept a steady, controlled volume. "Do you think it could hold a job? Do you think it could raise a family, or make the big decisions a person has to make in a life, the decisions a human life forces a person to make?"

Sam at first had been standing a couple of feet behind Naomi, but he had gradually edged sideways, toward the corner of the room, to a place where he wasn't close to anyone. But he wasn't hiding behind anyone either. Naomi had told him he would have to speak up for himself. And now, ever so quietly, he started to speak. He had watched Carrie and now he was answering her question, was trying to answer it anyway.

"Ah ink ah cud. Ah ink ah cud do at. Es." It was a small series of sounds, and even Naomi did not hear all of it; Carrie certainly heard nothing, she was in full flight now, a flight she could not control.

"You think Sam could act like a human, take on responsibilities as a human does?" It was a rhetorical question, of course, and addressed to Naomi, but again a little voice from off to one side answered as if it had been real.

"Ah no ah cud." His voice was hushed, so much so that you could hardly hear it, and the trouble he had enunciating did not make it any easier. Again Carrie could not pick out the sounds, but this time Naomi heard clearly, and she started to jump up and down.

"*Listen*, Mommy, you have to *listen*! You're not hearing me, you're not hearing Sam, you just don't care what I'm saying, what he says, you're just . . ." Sam thought of Kanga when Piglet had said *I am not Roo, I am Piglet* and Kanga had kept right on treating him as Roo until Piglet had shouted *Can't you see? Haven't you got eyes? Look at me!* And then it was all right, Kanga had been just pretending. Could Carrie be pretending too?

"That's *enough*!" Carrie really had had enough. Her daughter was a sweet child, and Sam was sweet too in his own way, but for God's sake he was a pet, a *pet*. Months ago, more than a year ago even, she should have put a stop to this, should have insisted, no matter what the child said. Naomi was putting her whole life into this creature, it had never been right and now it was worse, she had become delusional, truly delusional. "I've been thinking of nothing but you all along, Naomi, you may not appreciate that now but in a few years . . . I can't expect you to understand now, you're a good child, you're a wonderful child, you make your mother proud and I love you more than anything, but a child can't understand everything, Naomi, a grown-up can't understand everything either, I know that, but there are even more things a child can't understand. I know you're going to find this very difficult, but it can't go on, that's all I can say, you and Sam, it just can't be allowed to continue."

"But Mommy, you can't mean . . ."

"I *do* mean. I told you right at the beginning that you had to act responsibly if you were to have a mongrel. I thought that 'act responsibly' would just mean you would need to take the time to care for a pet properly. That's what I tried to drill into you and you've done that, it's to your credit. You've been responsible in those sorts of ways, responsible beyond your years. I just never thought—maybe I should have thought, but I didn't—that you would give up your friends, I didn't think you'd start to go so crazy about a pet mongrel that you'd start to think it was human. It just never crossed my mind that being responsible in that sort of way would be an issue.

I'm so sorry, Gnome, I don't know what to say." How could she console her daughter in the midst of such devastation? All this was more Zayne's department, really—consolation, the soft things. But it would be days rather than hours before he would be back from New York. "Maybe we can get you another," she offered, "maybe get you another one after a few months or so. But this one . . ." she looked at Sam with compassion but also with something of the distaste she had never quite extinguished, "this one has to go."

"Mommy! You can't! Mommy, he can be your little boy, he can be my brother, Mommy, no no no, you mustn't, you can't," and then there was only frantic sobbing; Naomi rushed back upstairs to her room, a stricken Sam pattering along in her wake. It took some time for Carrie to compose herself. She wanted to rush after her daughter and offer her love in some way, as she had when Naomi had been just a very little gnome. But she forced herself to stay where she was, she knew that the girl should be given some time to regain control, to come to her senses. It was well over an hour later that Carrie stood outside the door to her daughter's room. It was hard to be calm but she told herself that calmness was worth striving for, that calmness would help to get them both through. And then, as she opened the door and looked at her little one all curled up, a warm wash of feeling spread through her. A feeling of love, there could be no other word for it. It was a mother's duty to be firm too, to set limits, to shape a child, to do the right thing, and to show a child what the right thing was, but it was so hard sometimes, so very hard. Slowly Carrie placed a hug around the quivering figure of her daughter. It would pass; it always did, she knew that, but oh, the pain that sometimes had to be gone through before it did.

Naomi felt something she had never felt before, something she did not have a name for. Her mouth was open to the air and yet she felt smothered, felt as if she had to squirm away somehow, to run and never to stop running, she never wanted to hear her mother again, never wanted to see her, never wanted to feel her, never wanted the touch of their bodies pressed together, those arms around her like a vice. How can you know something and be so wrong? It couldn't be, it just couldn't!

Sam was younger, but he knew very well that such things could be. He had no thought of running, there was no place to run, this wasn't at all like little Piglet running with the balloon and he fell and it burst but it was all right in the end. When things took a turn like this there was nothing you could do to try to make it be right in the end. You could only be wishing, but sometimes wishing could bring a bright day, maybe sometimes it could, a new day and a bright one. Naomi sometimes sang a song with those words in it, he had seen them on her lips often. What was a tune? A tune always went with words when it was a song, Sam knew nothing of music except that it was. That was all. And he knew that Naomi's eyes would always turn upward when she sang, and a light would come into them, a brighter light, there was always a light there, she was everything bright to him, and now he was going to lose her, he mustn't think about that, maybe maybe maybe, sometimes a new day sometimes a bright day you never know, never, no one ever knows how it will end and maybe, maybe a nice walk after supper, maybe far longer than usual by the river, she would take him for a nice walk, maybe she would take him as she always did, just him and Naomi, Naomi and him, he loved her so much, mustn't think, mustn't think.

What exactly was to be done with it? That was the question. Carrie could imagine the ongoing hysterics if they took it to the Repository, with all the questions, all the doubts about who would claim him, what sort of home he would go to. If Naomi was near hysterical now, what would be her state after days of that? And if they did manage to find out what other family had claimed it, Carrie could hardly imagine the intensity and the persistence of *please can we visit, please can we see him? Mommy, Daddy, we have to!* But if they took Sam to the Repository and no one claimed him, that might well be more difficult still. Naomi would be phoning every day, checking to see if someone had adopted it, to see if it was okay. If the three-week deadline approached and it still had not been claimed—which was to say, if it was about to be sent off to the chattel farm, the Repositories made it quite clear what happened at that stage, they could not keep an animal indefinitely—well, no mother would want to inflict those feelings on her daughter.

For a fleeting moment Carrie thought of doing once more to the creature exactly what had been done to it in the first place, when it had arrived out of nowhere on their doorstep. Why not? If it were on the other side of town this time, or perhaps on some doorstep in a good neighborhood in Hanover or Wakefield, two or three towns away, what were the chances of it ever being . . . of Naomi ever seeing it? But no, if whatever family it was decided to keep the creature, and if they did ever happen to run into the Stinsons on the street or in the park or wherever, how could Carrie possibly explain it? Explain it to the other family, explain it most of all to Naomi? Her daughter would be sure to rush up, be sure to hug the creature and kiss it and cry, the parents would inevitably get into conversation, and the whole embarrassing thing would have to come out. If Naomi were ever to discover that Carrie had abandoned Sam, had just taken the thing somewhere and left it, she would never forgive her mother, never.

And there was the tag, as well. Not the metal tag on the collar ring, the tag that you attached to the leash and that had Sam's name on it. That would obviously present no difficulty; it could simply be removed. No, the problem would be the code tattooed inside the ear. They had used to do the same to dogs and cats in the old days, the days before the great extinctions, and now every mongrel had one, or was supposed to have one at any rate, so that if it got lost it could be easily identified. Poor families often did without and risked the fine; Sam had been without a tattoo when he'd been left on their doorstep. But that had been one of the first things they'd done once they had decided they would keep him. No, leaving it on a doorstep would never do, if she left it on a doorstep the family would see the tattoo, would find out with one call who the creature belonged to; they would all be right back where they started, except with even more trouble and awkwardness, right back with Naomi spending all her time with the creature.

A wave of feeling began to sweep through Carrie. She was under its control, under it utterly, and she felt driven toward action. Whatever it might be, she felt driven to do something now. All this time she'd let things drift, let everything go further and further, and now there could be no more drifting, no more wait and see and hope for the best. Was there really only one choice when it came down to it? There were places, there were people, things could be done. They weren't entirely respectable and she wasn't sure everything they did was entirely legal but she knew it wasn't entirely illegal either, and she didn't think that the places and the people would be all that difficult to find. They weren't directly connected to the chattel farms, she was pretty sure of that, she thought they usually called themselves "facilitators," they were probably in the directory, it would be simple to look them up.

And it was indeed as simple as that; she jotted down an address, a number to call, probably she would never use it but you never knew, she would like not to have to think of the choices, none of them was a good choice but any mother would feel she had to do something if it were her daughter.

If Zayne were here—no, maybe it was better that Zayne was away. It would not be until late in the evening that he would be back, he had decided to stay over in New York for two or three days after the opening, with every show it seemed there was more for him to do, more buyers to be wined and dined with the gallery owners or managers. It had been like that ever since that first New York show six years ago when the *Times* had *oohed* and *aahed* about the purity of his sense of color, his boldness. No, if Zayne were here it would only confuse things, he wouldn't be *against* doing anything but he wouldn't be in favor of anything either, *Why don't we just let things ride for a while?* he would say. *Let's hope for the best*, he would say that too, he always did. And that's exactly what they'd been doing all this time, and where had it gotten them? Who knew what sort of psychological damage they had caused already to the child? No, Zayne would be no help at a time like—

"Mommy." The small voice came at her from the kitchen doorway. "Mommy, I love you Mommy." She must have come downstairs ever so quietly, Carrie had not heard a sound. And she had brought Sam with her, there he was again, just behind her, "I love you Mommy and I know you want me to stay in my room but this is too important,

Mommy, I have to try and make you understand." Her face was still red, but she was not crying now, and nor was Sam behind her. She looked at her mother's face—it was neither soft nor hard, you couldn't tell how it would go. "Just listen to me, Mommy, please listen, but mostly listen to *him*, listen to Sam, you're not giving him a chance." If she had said *not giving me a chance* it might all have turned the other way, but now Naomi was pushing all the wrong buttons, it was already like a hothouse the way the two of them . . ., no it was not healthy, it was not right, it would stop here and now.

"All *right*! Sam, you come with me. Sam, come!" She accompanied the words with vigorous but awkward gestures, her mind racing like an engine that was being revved but that was stuck in too low a gear. Yes, it was time to separate the two of them. Taking him anywhere was better than having him stay here. Anywhere, and then she could collect her thoughts. Keep him away from Naomi, that was the main thing, this had absolutely gone too far.

"Where are you going, Mommy? Where are you taking him?"

"I don't know, Naomi, I honestly don't know. I have to think through what's best, and if I'm going to do that I have to know that whatever weirdness has gone on with you and Sam isn't continuing. Until I figure out what to do, the two of you can just stay apart, you're eleven now, you'll be perfectly fine on your own for a few hours if that's what it takes, there's plenty of food in the refrigerator."

"Mommy! You're not thinking right, Mommy, I love you Mommy but you can't, really Mommy, you're getting everything all turned around, you . . ." Now Carrie had Sam by the wrist and was pulling him along with her. "Mommy, I hate you, why can't you *listen*!" The words were out of Naomi's mouth before she even knew it. Where had they come from? She wanted them to be squished back into her, wanted to forget they had ever come out. Her mother stared at her as if she were in another place, as if her look came from another place. Something had gone missing inside her. *Mommy what's happened what's happened?*

And then they were gone, the wheels screeching a little on the driveway, *gone where?* "I'll be back when I'm back," she had said. "I will figure out what's best to do, that's what grown-ups have to do,

Naomi, they have to sort things out, and sometimes they don't get any thanks for it. Or any *love*," she had added with fierce emphasis as she had closed the door of the car. She had not wanted to say that, but that was what had come out and the windows were up, the engine was revving, there had been no time for Naomi to say *I do love you, Mommy, I do I do*, no time and no air.

Carrie drove almost aimlessly for several minutes. The shops had closed already on Water Street where she liked to get that special coffee. The rush hour had passed but there were still many people about, on their way home after work, most of them. Even before all this it had been a strange day for Carrie, staying home with Zayne away, and the school holidays, Naomi home too. How did he cope with it, being in the house all the time? Of course he had his studio, and being able to spend time in the garden was always nice—look, there were Peter and Meg Sullivan on the sidewalk, they had seen her, they were waving and she waved back distractedly, they were just living their normal lives, maybe that was what she should do, maybe that would help her to focus, just pretend it was a normal day. They were low on orange juice, crackers, they could use some more of that olive dip, maybe some fruit cocktail as well, Foodway would still be open, she would just stop in there and maybe her mind would clear, she could focus. She pulled into the parking lot, it was still bustling, people picking up things on the way home for their dinner, she couldn't leave Sam in the car, it was still so warm it would be like a furnace, she grabbed the leash from the glove compartment and clicked it onto his collar, she could leave him clipped to that rail by the main entrance, he would not run off, no, he might sense danger but he would sense too that the greater danger would be as a stray. The juice, crackers, olive dip, maybe some of those little sausages Zayne loved so much, Naomi would never eat those but perhaps a small package, no, no, something made her turn away, she didn't need any of that. She needed to focus, the crackers, maybe some of that good vodka to go with the fruit cocktail, at the end of the long day Zayne sometimes liked some vodka on ice, they hadn't had any in the house for a long time but yes, just a small bottle, that gray one, God, she could use a drink herself sometimes, Zayne used to always say after those times at the lake that it wasn't good for her but sometimes everyone needed something to help them relax, get a grip on things. It wasn't as if she'd ever really embarrassed him those weekends at the lake either, or embarrassed herself, for that matter. Really there hadn't been any problem except maybe in Zayne's mind. Anyway right now the thing was to focus on what had to be done, she had been avoiding things, what had to be done? Did it really need to be done? If it did she was the one who had to do it, there could be no question about that—*Thank you, yes, that's right, no, no Foodway card today, yes lovely, isn't it, but a bit cooler would be nice*, and then there he was outside, he hadn't gone away, it was still her problem.

"Isn't he cute? Isn't he lovely?" the woman was saying, it was Sam she was looking at, "Isn't he just lovely?"

Naomi was holding back her tears, her mother didn't like it if she cried, she knew that, some mothers and fathers would do anything you wanted if you cried, but not Carrie.

"Well," offered Zayne. "I'm sure your mother was trying to think of what was best." He was still trying to take in something of what had happened, how everything had suddenly turned; he had only just gotten in from the airport. He wanted to show Carrie he wasn't against her, it wasn't true what she'd said about him the other day. He knew it was important to have a united front as parents but he could hear that his words sounded awkward, tinny, it was all awkward and something had happened and it had been Carrie's doing. They would have a lot of sorting out to do, he and Carrie, that much was plain. But that could wait. What had happened here? What exactly had happened?

"I *was* thinking of what was best! You two both know perfectly well that once you have met people you can sometimes feel confident that they . . . Well, I *did* meet some people." She was not lying; all this had happened exactly as she was telling them. "A couple coming out of the grocery store, they just looked at it as I was unleashing it."

Why was she calling Sam *it*, Zayne suddenly wondered. She had hardly ever done that since the first days after they had taken him in.

". . . And they smiled and said, 'Isn't he lovely? Isn't he lovely?' They kept saying it, both of them, as if it was a thought that kept occurring to each of them independently. And little Sammy looked up at them all big-eyed, he really looked as if he liked them, believe me I was paying attention to that. Just let me finish, let me tell you how it all happened.

"'Do you behave yourself around the house?' That's what the woman asked. 'Are you a little rascal?' she said, 'a little cutie, a little cutie rascal?'

"'Dear,' her husband said, he didn't seem quite so taken by Sam, 'we should be getting along and leaving this lady to . . .' or something like that, I can't remember exactly what he said. But then the wheels started to turn for me. 'Do you have one yourself?' I asked them.

"'No children, no pets,' said the man, he was friendly but it seemed he really did want to get to where they were both going. And then he moved a little away, he started looking away too, he wasn't really paying attention. Perhaps he was far enough away not to hear, but still, I could hardly believe what the woman said to me next.

"'I'd *love* to have a little mongrel. Ralph and I can't have children, that's the fact of it. I don't know why I'm telling you this.' And then she looked at her husband, he was several feet away now. 'Ralph would never want me to tell a stranger what I just told you, but, but I'd love it, I really would. You're very lucky!' And I told her I was lucky, I told her that my husband and my daughter and I were all lucky, but I said that sometimes . . ."

"Did you give him to them, Mommy? You gave him to them, didn't you?" A thing inside Naomi tightened and held and twisted, it hurt her, she could hardly breathe for a moment, what was it her mother had said?

Carrie knew she would have to be so careful now with what she said so as not to hurt Naomi, not any more than she was hurting already, it must be so hard what the child was going through. The last thing she wanted to do was in any way add to that. She could lessen the pain if she had just the right words, just the right story, but it was so hard to be careful with every word when the strings of her heart kept thrumming like this. "What I *said* to them," she repeated, "was that there can sometimes be uncertainty or confusion about what the right path is for everybody, if you have both a mongrel and a child of a certain age in the same household. If it's an only child and she stops seeing any of her friends and her pet becomes her only friend and she starts to get strange ideas—I didn't say all that to them, but I said it can be better to be a pet in a household that wants a pet and where there wouldn't ever be any issues over having a pet."

Then she turned to her husband. "Zayne, I know I should have talked this through with you first, I guess I lost my head a little, but I know it's the best thing for Naomi, for all of us really." She had been able to snatch only a brief moment with him before this, she had told him quickly that Naomi had gone almost hysterical and had begun to think Sam was human, that Carrie had felt she'd had to act—there had been no time to tell him more. She turned again to their daughter. "That's what I truly believe, Naomi. That's what both your parents believe." She looked at Zayne from the side of her eye; probably he believed no such thing, how could he when he hadn't been there, hadn't seen it? But would he break with her; would he side with the child against her?

"You did give him to them, I know you did!" Naomi looked back and forth from one parent to the other.

"I don't know if your mother . . ." Zayne faltered. What was there he could say? How could Carrie put him in this situation? She knew perfectly well how he felt. This was her doing, all of it. Oh, they'd agreed about the importance of parents keeping a united front before the children, sure, but this . . . What exactly had happened earlier in the day? He couldn't make head or tail of it. The show had gone so well, everything had sold this year, Carrie hadn't even asked him about that but it had been a sea of red dots, he would really be able to make a contribution financially for the first time since—anyway, it had all seemed fine here, he had spoken to Carrie the night before, everything had seemed fine. How could it all suddenly be so upside down? She'd said Naomi had somehow lost it; he would have to take that at face value, he supposed, but it was all he could do not to contradict Carrie openly. He twisted and kept his lips tight. His eyes were fixed grimly on his shoes. His sentence remained unfinished as the red spread across his cheeks, his neck, his forehead. Naomi was making little gasping noises, as if she were trying to cry and it couldn't happen somehow, there was no air for that.

Carrie kept thinking this was so hard, and the thing inside her was tight with something like pain, but it was for the best, this was all for the best, this was how it had to be. And maybe she wouldn't even need to lie. Wouldn't that be a sign that she had done the right thing, that she had carried through courageously with a difficult choice, and that it had been the right choice? It would have been so easy to have caved in and told them more than they needed to know; so often in life it took strength to do what was right.

They seemed to have inferred the rest of the story—maybe that was for the best, too—and to have moved on to the large issues at stake, to be preoccupied even more than Carrie had imagined they would be by the simple fact of Sam not being with them any more. Naomi was saying it wasn't fair, it wasn't fair, and Zayne was saying nothing to contradict her. "Naomi, Naomi," Carrie said, "so much isn't fair. I thought it was fair that a family with no child, a family that can't have a child, be able to have something like Sam in the household. Don't you think that's fair? Maybe not now, Naomi, but some day I think you'll understand, some day I think you'll understand about all different sorts of fairness and how difficult it is to know what's right, to do what's right. Your mommy and daddy know how difficult it is for you now. It's so hard, but it will get better, really it will. Your mother and daddy love you, you know that, you know your daddy loves you, and your mommy loves you too."

Carrie had always found it sloppy the way her own mother—even her father—had said this sort of thing when she was a child. "I love you," her mommy would always say when she tucked Carrie into bed, even when she was as old as twelve, thirteen. It was with that in mind that Carrie had always sought a better formula, one that made plain the presence of affection—a child needed affection, you had to recognize that—but that didn't let it get too personal, too gushy. "You know your mommy loves you" was the formula she had begun to use when Naomi was very young. Sometimes it was hard to keep from saying more, from being more effusive, smothering, but from the first time she had used it she had known immediately from the powerful grip of her daughter's little hands as Naomi had hugged Carrie in response that she had gotten it just right.

Naomi would go off to bed now, and no doubt she would cry herself to sleep. But in a few days, in a few weeks certainly, it would be all right. Everything would be all right, wouldn't it? Suddenly Carrie felt as helpless as her daughter, *What had happened? What had happened? Had it really happened?*

It had all happened just as Carrie had said, every word she had said was true. She *had* thought of letting the nice couple take Sam away, and she had maybe said something to the woman like "that would be wonderful all round." But the husband had been impatient and suspicious when he had drifted back toward them. The conversation had jerked awkwardly to a close, and Carrie had felt like kicking herself for her impetuousness. Of *course* it wouldn't be for the best to let them take Sam, she knew that as soon as she began to think it through. All the issues that would have been raised if she had taken the creature to the Repository or left it anonymously on a doorstep were just as relevant here.

What the little incident had given her was only a story, something for Naomi to believe, maybe even Zayne. She had realized almost as soon as the couple had moved on that she would still have to do the difficult thing, the thing she had dreaded, that her trip with Sam was not over.

Afterward, when it *was* really over, she had to go over everything in her mind, everything from the incident outside the grocery store especially, for that was the story she would have to tell, that was the story she would have to get straight in her mind, there was no point in dwelling on anything about the rest of the trip, of what had happened then. It was so hard to think, so hard to think anything, but she forced herself to focus on just how to tell everything, how to make it real, the childless couple, the little details, the very words they had used. If she used their words again, that would bring it to life, she knew it would. The rest of it she never wanted to think of again. Never. There are things in life that everyone has to do, just a few things that they never want to think of again, that they should never have to think of again.

Maybe I should say something, Sam had kept thinking as Carrie had been talking to Ralph and his wife. *Maybe if I say something I could say the (right) thing, the thing that would make it right.* But none of the right words were in him, he could only think *help, help* like Piglet with the Heffalump crying out and scampering off, there had been no Heffalump, the fear had been only in little Piglet's mind, and it had been all right, but Sam could not say *help*, he could not say anything, all the words were stuck inside him, and he said nothing until Ralph and his wife had moved on, and Carrie had undone his leash and walked him over to the car, and put him in the backseat just as if it were any other day. But he knew it was not any other day. On any normal day Carrie would never have brought him along unless Naomi were coming too, unless Naomi had pleaded with her to bring him too, that was the way it always was. Today had been so different, so sad and so different, and now Sam felt a tightening, it was like only one thing, like the last time with his family, his true family, when he didn't yet know but he knew, it was like that now.

Almost as soon as they were out of the store's parking lot Carrie pulled over. It was a residential street, a bit of a backwater. There was no one on the sidewalk but Sam saw her glance around and then pull a gray plastic bottle from the grocery bag, quickly twist it open, and put it to her lips. Sam saw her throat jerk several times, and saw her mouth move like people do when they are gasping after they have finished drinking. She did not look at him then, it was as if he were not there. She rummaged in her handbag and pulled out a tangle of paper, unfolded it and jerked at it as if it were resisting her, but she seemed quickly to find what she needed. Then she half folded, half crumpled the map back into the pocket. She started the car again, but from the way she turned at the end of the block Sam knew they were not going back home, not going back to Zayne and to Naomi, *Where were they going?* When Max had been sent to bed without any supper he had gone to where the wild things were and then there had been a wild rumpus but when Max had wanted to stop he said stop and it had stopped and the wild things had cried "Oh please don't go" but he had sailed back to his very own room with the supper his mother had made waiting for him and it was still warm, please could it be like that?

They drove and they drove until the city thinned out, scrawny little bungalows with no curtains, a run-down old canning factory, low warehouses, vacant lots. It was dusk.

"Mehbeh u cud ake me u ma muddah."

"Of course I can't take you to your mother. I have no idea where she is, to start with." It was not until Carrie had finished answering him that a flash of astonishment swept over her. What had she thought she was hearing? Of course some of them could understand a good deal, even put together a few words of their own, she had always accepted that, and perhaps he was a little better than most of them, she had always noticed that his forehead was not quite so . . . That didn't make Naomi right, the girl was clearly confused, but Carrie felt suddenly the sharp pull of having done wrong: she should not have shouted, she should have dealt with it differently, been calmer, and now Naomi hated her. *Oh God what had she done, what had she done?* Could her little gnome have been right all along? The thing was so like a human, *Oh my God Oh my God*, but no, it couldn't be, those eyes—even if it were, could she ever take it back? And take back everything she had said? Take all that back, given everything Sam had been doing with Naomi, given everything they *must* have been doing together? It made no sense otherwise: why would the two of them have been spending all that time together? No, you couldn't go back, there were times in life when you just had to go on, had to not think, when you had to just go forward. And what did it matter now? There was no one else around who would hear, there would be no one else. She couldn't think straight, she could barely feel, but she began to talk.

"Your mother abandoned you, remember? Or someone abandoned you, at any rate. If we'd known where we could return you, you can be sure I would have returned you there and then." There was silence, and then a tiny whimpering. It was getting dark now; Carrie switched on the headlights. She would have to focus too on just where they were going; she hardly ever headed out of town in this direction. And then words started again to come from her mouth. "All right! I know it's not your fault, none of it is. But it isn't about you, not really. I don't know what sort of creature you are, I don't think I know anything at all, really. And I don't feel right about this now, believe me I don't, but I haven't felt right about any of it from the start. It was true what I said about you and Naomi, it isn't natural, it *isn't*, it's not good for her. *You're* not good for her."

It didn't matter in the end what he was. It all came down to that: was he good for her? Was he good for the three of them, Zayne and Naomi and her? It had been a world of three people, happy enough for the most part, a world with enough money for them all, more than enough, and no heartaches. If a boy, a boy that was not Zayne's, were added to it, a boy that Naomi had been . . . , no, she would not go there again. "I won't have it, that's all there is to it. I just won't." She hunched forward over the wheel. She was speaking to herself, really, but Sam strained forward a bit from the backseat, forward and a bit to one side; he could see her lips in the mirror. She was not making any effort to speak slowly, he thought, but her thoughts were coming slowly; he could pick up most of it. Inside himself, he wondered simple things: *Why does it hurt so much? When will she take me home?* And then Carrie began to speak again to him.

"My husband—Zayne . . ." she added, oddly, as though Zayne were a distant relative of hers. "He was married once before. We had both had relationships with other people, of course, it wasn't as if we were virgins"—why on earth had she put it that way, she wondered—"but he had actually been married. He has a child, a son. When Zayne and I met I was not very good about . . . I was not very good, that's all. I told him he could have me, he could have me forever, but only if he could accept that I couldn't have his child around us. I knew, I thought I knew, it would spoil things between us. And it would spoil things with whatever children we had, the two of us.

It all seemed so delicate, dangerous even." She paused again, and glanced in the mirror at the creature, staring at her, the whimpering now slower, quieter. "So you see I can't say yes now to this sort of thing, I can't have some new thing added to the family as if it were a son. You see that, don't you? I turned down his own boy, you see that, don't you? I can't . . ." She was whimpering herself now, tears kept sliding steadily down from her eyes.

"El av me illd. Yor oing u let em ill me." Sam's little voice made the sounds flat and soft, pressed down by something inside him.

"Look, you're not a bad creature, I can see that. Maybe you'll find some way out. I just know I can't find it for you. Your mother should have realized there can be complications. You can't just plunk a creature down on people's doorsteps and be sure it's going to be all right. She should have thought of that!" Carrie was flailing, she couldn't think straight. When she came to her senses later, she would no more believe what she was saying now about Tammy than she would believe that any of it was Sam's fault.

There was a long pause as they drove through the night. The streets were empty, the heat had broken into thunderstorms, the road was slick now with rain. "It's so dark," she whispered, "it's so dark out here." She flipped on the overhead light and peered again at the scrap of paper as she drove. "I don't want to be here," she whispered, "I want it to be over, I want to be home." Maybe it was no more than momentum now, but she kept driving, she forced herself to pay attention to the numbers of the houses, the few of them where there was enough light to see, a little light by the door or a streetlamp close enough to cast its light on a number. She was driving east, and the numbers were going down—12812, 12804, and then they were there. A nondescript, low gray bungalow with a concrete porch, the paint peeling on the white trim, set well back from the street. It didn't look like anything, really, certainly not like any proper business, there wasn't even a sign. Could there have been some mistake? She looked again at the piece of paper, crumpled now, she had jotted the number down quickly. Some people might reverse two digits in a number that long, but not Carrie, that was the sort of mistake she hardly ever made.

The rain was harder now, falling in sheets, as she opened the back door. She would just make sure that the address wasn't a mistake before they drove off, before she had to think of some different plan. Maybe it would be for the best if it—but she was here now, *they* were here now, she took Sammy's hand as she helped him out of the backseat, *helped*, that might have been the word you used usually, but this time he shrank back a little, *Could you blame him, really?* she thought. The poor thing, she knew it wasn't his fault, it wasn't anyone's fault really, so many things weren't anyone's fault. But that didn't make them right, and you had to deal with them, you had to keep dealing with them as best you could, otherwise life always felt like it would take a corner too fast and go off the rails. Of course she hadn't brought an umbrella, they both started to get soaked very quickly as they scrambled up the walk to the porch. The concrete of the walk was cracked and uneven, she would remember that later for some reason, was Sam gripping her hand tightly or was it the other way round?

In this part of town she knew no one, in the heavy rain no one would see or hear anything anyway. For a moment those thoughts seemed to calm her, she did not quite know why but that was only for a moment, probably there would be no one home—was it a business or a home, or both?—her hair was tangled in wet mats there was a small sound beside her in amongst the sounds of the wind and the rain and then a runny face peering through the wet little window in the weather-beaten door, there was someone there after all.

The corners of the room were dark, and he could not quite make out the shapes along the walls. Machines of some sort? Garden tools? Sam tried to give them shape. He did not want to think of the man Carrie had left him with, with his plump, factual face. "We have to just put these on him, a matter of form is all," the man had said to Carrie as he had twisted Sam's little top limbs behind his back and slipped the standard Jenkins' restraint system over them. And then the heavy cloth had dropped over his head. Then there was a short time, or maybe it was not a very short time, maybe he had slept just a little, he was so tired. And then the cloth had been pulled away and Sam had started to try to figure out where he could be. They had taken him outside after Carrie had left, he could feel the warm night air, but they had stood around him as they walked him forward so that nothing would be visible to anyone passing. They had pushed him—thrown him, almost—into the back of a van, and then they had started driving. He thought there were two of them in the front. Then a few steps forward, and then down some steps, he could see almost nothing it was so dim. It smelled like a cellar. And then a thick door opened and another door but this time a thin one, metal, he was in some cage. Maybe he slept again, he did not know, then another click, hands wrenching him from the cage and to his feet, push push pushing him into—into what? Where was he? It wasn't quite so dim now, he could see he was in a room, the corners were dark, but suddenly a bright light shone on his head, on the left side of his head, the hands were on him again, holding him, and some sort of clamp was lowered from a fixture bolted to the ceiling. They fixed it around his skull just above the ears, he did not want to look at their lips but he could not stop himself. One of the men peered at the numbers on Sam's left ear—tattooed numbers just like any mongrel had, that is if the owners were responsible, if they'd had it registered. His were 414-B3; 414 was coded for the district and the last part, B3, was coded for a specific veterinary clinic.

If it was a human tattoo and you wanted it removed there were special ways of doing that but they were highly time-consuming ways, and expensive too. You would never do it that way with an animal.

"It's this thing's bad luck that they got it registered, isn't it? But there's no getting round it, the farms can't take in any registered mongrels, there's no wiggle room on that one. No pets, not unless it's put through as part of the euthanasia program, and everything properly documented, mind, it's all a firm rule." That was the older one of the two talking; maybe he was explaining things to the younger one, maybe more to himself. "But you got to see that lady's point of view too. Trouble. What with the kid, and the way the kid and the pet were acting, can't expect a family to stand for that on and on. And that's where we can help. But no joy for this creature," he murmured as the blade sliced down, "no joy at all."

The apprentice flinched at the animal's scream, and the young man felt a twitching in some muscles in his chest. How could he ever get used to this? But the money, he had promised himself he would stick with it for now, his parents kept saying he should go back to school, but what was the point, really? And the truck and all that, he'd got it all for the lawn care business, it had sounded like such a great opportunity but so few people had lawns any more, bushes and cacti and woodchips had just about taken over, so that hadn't worked, but still he had the truck, there'd be no way he'd be able to keep up the payments if he didn't . . . he'd stick with it for now, anyway.

"See how cleanly it comes off?" The old hand held up the ear, neatly sheared off, right at the base. "No registration number on this one now, is there?" he asked in grim triumph. The shrieks had scarcely let up, but the apprentice was even now starting to get used to the volume a little. "All you need to do is take one of these . . ." said the old hand, pulling the thick gauze wad from a large box, "douse it with antiseptic"—here again he suited his words to actions—"and clamp it down." With a series of motions he loosened the head clamp enough to slip it a little lower, pressed the gauze on the place where the ear had been attached, and re-tightened it. "Just two hours like that, and it'll be ready for delivery."

PART

3

Carrie had known within minutes that she had done something horribly wrong. For a moment she tried to tell herself no, she had only *allowed* something horribly wrong to be done, there was a difference between the two and a person didn't need to be harder on herself than she deserved. Which was true, but when the backwash from the storm surge of feeling pulled at her she knew with complete clarity that everything had gone appallingly wrong, that she had turned it all appallingly wrong, and the knowledge seemed to grip something inside of her, locking on like pliers just below her heart. The next day and the day after and the day after that it was still there, and the next week, and two and three weeks later. But then every week it became a little less tight as time began to do its work of softening, easing. Maybe time would have the power to forgive.

It was on a Sunday morning that it suddenly struck Carrie; she had not felt the locking inside her for maybe a day, maybe even two days. And for a few seconds a new wave flowed through her, a surge of relief, and with it a sense of gratitude. But just as suddenly came again a feeling of wrongness, but one of a different color, a conviction that the tightly locked feeling *belonged* inside her, that she deserved to have that feeling within herself. Losing it now, escaping, was too easy. The relief and the gratitude sank away as if through thin and sandy soil. Emptied, she stood up and walked with strange deliberation to the dining room.

The house was quiet, with the same strange, tense quiet that had prevailed through most of the days since that awful night. Zayne had some papers spread out on the dining room table. He was working on their taxes, he always did the taxes for both of them. Naomi was upstairs in her room. Almost always these days she stayed in her room—who knew what she was doing or thinking? But maybe it was better for her that way, maybe she had to go through her anger and her resentment and all that, though it was strange how un-angry

Naomi seemed. How could you tell what she was feeling? Surely she *should* be angry. Didn't they always say that there was a stage you had to go through, a stage when it was better to be left alone? Carrie was pretty sure it was for the best that Naomi was keeping mostly to herself these days. And as she watched her husband hunched over his numbers, happy enough for perhaps the last time in a very long time, Carrie knew too with certainty that it was for the best that her daughter was not there with them right at that moment. If Naomi had been there Carrie could not have brought herself to say what she was being pushed toward saying, what some strange calm force that came from a place she did not know was pushing her toward saying. Zayne would tell Naomi afterward, she supposed. He would feel he'd have to tell her, no doubt. But just at this moment it was something for the two of them, and that made it easier. Zayne had a surprising capacity for anger and for bitterness, Carrie had come to know that about him. He would never be able to do terrible things as she had done, but nor could he do as much that was good. What he could do was resent the bad things that other people did, and stay off to one side. He would resent this most of all, she knew that perfectly well. But maybe not just resent it quietly, maybe this time the feeling would be strong enough that he would do something about it. It would be not such a bad thing if he ended what there was between them. And maybe it would make him feel things a little more meaningfully, a little more deeply; he had never been one for deep or complex feelings, her Zayne. Not much capacity for action, not much capacity for elation or anguish or despair, either. Zayne was the odd one in the family, really—that was not how it was with Naomi, or how it was with her. Carrie stood there for half a minute more, resting her shoulder on the doorframe, wondering how much she knew of this person in front of her with a pencil, entirely absorbed with some arithmetical operation. She waited for him to notice her, to turn, and then the words began to come out of her mouth.

"Zayne, I have to tell you something. I have done something very wrong." And from there it was much easier, all the rest had a momentum to it. It was not that doing the right thing now made what she had done earlier any less wrong, or that she thought she would be forgiven or redeemed. None of that would be possible, she knew well enough what folly and emptiness there could be in those sorts of delusions. It was just the momentum. Should you even call it that, or was it inertia when something had begun to move, and would just keep moving? Naomi would know, young as she was.

And Zayne, what of him? As she kept telling the story to him Carrie saw him as if from far away, the expressions flying across his face like the shadows of clouds across the plain. Across the plain as a gale approaches—gusts of disbelief, of horror, of shock, of fury. And then a frenzy, Zayne running and screaming past her, up the stairs, blurting out the gist of everything to Naomi and barking instructions to her, to Carrie, the one who until now he had looked up to so steadily, had relied on to take the lead.

There were things that she would now have to do, things that she had known would be necessary, right from the moment he had turned to her and the words had begun to come from her mouth. They would go back to that house, the three of them, the gray house with the peeling trim. They would find where Sam had been taken and what had been done to him, they would save him. *Save.* The sound of the word spread and dissipated like an echo in mist. But they would do whatever could be done, Zayne was telling Naomi just that, they would do whatever needed to be done, those were the words he used, it all sounded so brave, but maybe too much, as if effort alone could make what you wanted come true. It wasn't like that, Carrie knew it wasn't like that, it had never been like that, could never be like that, was not like that now. Her daughter knew that too: her child's face was ashen, this was beyond the worst she'd imagined.

Now Carrie suddenly saw Zayne as separate from her. She would go with him, perhaps even stay with him if that seemed right, but it was not fully a family now, most of that had drained away. It was her daughter she wanted to be with, stay with, this had all been done for Naomi. What would happen now, what could be made to happen now?

Zayne stumbled slightly as he moved toward the front door and the car outside, Naomi's wrist tight in his hand. He did not need to do that, Carrie thought; their daughter was desperate to come along with him. Carrie thought she could tell him as he drove where she had taken it—where she had taken Sam. She could show him just where, out on the Greeley Road. That was what was possible, that was all.

He could not escape the smell, it was everywhere, it got into everything. It was old sweat, it was rot, it was pee, but mostly it was the other one, the really smelly one that everyone did, but everyone should do it in private and here they had to do it where you could see, it was over a grate but you could see the turds bulging out as an animal squatted, most of it going through the grate usually, but always bits sticking to the skin around, bits flicking off on the ground, sometimes hard, sometimes drippy, and the smell—he couldn't bear it, he couldn't. Maybe he was better able to smell than the others were. Or maybe it smelled the same to all of them, he did not know. But he knew it was worse than anything, worse than the ear even, it didn't stop it, couldn't heal, he couldn't sleep, he always would turn and then be suddenly filled with it, right up in the middle of his head, he couldn't get it out. He would try to block it, he would tear little pieces of his coverall off and put them up his nose, for a little while it would be better but then the bits got sodden and were no good.

He didn't want to go himself, not ever over that grate, he could hold it in for the longest time and then sneak over to the grate in the middle of the night when he could hear the others sleeping, the snores, the regular breathing; then they would not see or smell what he did himself.

Even after being there for days he still did not know where he was, not really. It was a great pen with hundreds of them, that he could see, hundreds and hundreds and a barrier all round. Beyond that it was hard to know anything, hard to see anything even, every so often there were slats in the barrier but then there was another set of boards, offset by a few inches so you could hardly see anything; it looked like there were more pens on three other sides. On the fourth side you could see things, there was a building, a huge dark building; that was where you went when it ended is what Sammy thought.

Every morning a great gate in the side opposite the dark building would slide open. Most of them would be marched out then,
all except Sam and a few others, maybe they were new or somehow
special too, or maybe sick but almost all of them looked a bit sick, it
was hard to tell. Anyway, most of them would be lined up and then
would file out, through another pen and then out into fields, Sammy
could get a glimpse of that if he stood near the gate to one side. This
was one of the pens for chattels-in-use, not one for final finishing, but
Sammy had not yet been cleared for work as a chattel-in-use. Would
he be like the others here? He would try to talk to them when they
came back from the fields.

"Ow ar u? Ar u ere long?" he spoke awkwardly, acutely aware, as
he had never been with Naomi, how he could not make the sounds
quite right. "I jus got ere," he would continue. One time when he
was speaking to one of them who looked more alert than the others, more interested, he started to go a little bit further. "I was ith
som good peopol . . ." but then he had stopped. Had they been
good? Some of them had not been good when it had mattered. Not
the one who had controlled everything, in the end she had not been
very good. Why had she been able to do what she wanted? Why not
Zayne doing what he wanted? Why was he not so very strong? And
why couldn't everything have been as Naomi wanted, why couldn't
he have stayed with her?

Where was she? He wanted to be with her, she loved him, he
knew she loved him. Not like people did when they were grown up
or when they were starting to grow up but like people did all their
lives, that sort of love. Wasn't that what mattered? Lots of people
said that mattered. Some of them said nothing else mattered but was
it true, did they mean it? He had heard humans talk of that love,
normal humans, not mongrels, and of how it could be everything.
He had felt that from his mother, had felt it from Naomi, and now it
was gone, maybe for always.

Hardly any of the others in the pens seemed to understand him,
maybe they were different somehow. They would make sounds but
most would hardly look at him, they would look away as if they were
scared. Some of them would smile at him in a tired way but that was

all. There were only two or three who seemed to hear him and would say a few words back to him, but he found it hard to read their lips, they did not speak as Naomi did, or Zayne, or Carrie. Only there was one who he thought he could understand a little bit, one who was so friendly, Sam didn't know what to call him but he thought maybe he could call him Josh, his lips made a *shh* shape when Sammy asked him who he was. Did he have a name? Sometimes it was an *osh* instead of a *shh*, and he made sound shapes that seemed like *eat now* and *sleep now* and he always looked so tired but he tried to smile when he saw Sammy. When he looked at anyone he would try to smile and sometimes he would hug Sammy, sometimes he would hug anyone, it just seemed that he needed that. Maybe they were all needing that but they were strangers and it seemed most of them were not like Josh, they looked so grim, it was always so hard for them, *no wonder, no wonder* thought Sammy.

One of the keepers spoke to them quite a lot, Sandie was her name. She came in the evenings and at night, *hello everyone* she would always say and then start yattering on about whatever was on her mind, just as if all of them could understand anything she said, just as if all of them were her friends. *Mouth open*, she would say to each one, she would always make the sounds clearly with her lips, Sam could understand every word. And *eyes wide*, and *right leg up* and then *left leg up*, and then she would move on to the next one. She would check every animal at least once each night; if some of the diseases took hold they could spread like anything, that's what she told Sammy when they got to talking. (She was always so pleased to hear someone really answer when she went through her list with each one. She told Sam she sometimes would start to feel it was habit that she spoke the instructions, part of the routine that helped keep her awake and alert. She knew perfectly well that most of them had no idea what she was saying, but she said she thought it helped them too, that they came to sense the order in which things were done, sometimes they would be lifting their feet in the right order even before she said the words. And once in a while, once in a long while, there would be a chattel like Sam that could understand everything she said and could say things back. When that happened Sandie found it would make her think not, *What a special one this is*, but, *Through this one I can feel something of what all of them must be feeling, all of them have hearts and minds, and I must never, never forget that*, that was most of all why it pleased her so much if she met one like Sam.)

Pinkeye was maybe the worst for spreading, except for foot-and-mouth, that was worse, but it was very rare or it had been very rare until it had started to spread from the laboratories where they were doing research. It had not been so bad when it only started from the animals themselves. But just on an everyday basis foot rot was maybe the worst. Certainly for the individual animal living day by day it was the worst of the common diseases, that was just because it was so hard to get rid of. "No wonder it's so common, it's all the feces, all that muck getting mixed in with the dirt, so the least little cut or scrape on the ball of the foot or between the toes or whatever, with any of that you get infection, you get fungi as well as bacteria, foot rot can go on and on for months. If it were a human they'd amputate but here . . ." She stopped then, she saw how Sam was watching her, it felt suddenly awkward, she had gone too far.

"Wat appens ere? Wat do ey do to them? U can tell me." Sam thought that he knew the answers to the questions he asked her, but he thought too it would be better to be sure, it would be worse not to know, that was what he told himself, but he wasn't sure that was true. He was only hoping.

"I guess you're going to find out anyway, perhaps it's not any worse if I . . ." She paused. "They're sent to the plant early, to the Special Processing Unit. That's what happens. They remove that limb first, or however much of it is diseased, and then the rest—well, you don't have to have all the details, I know you don't." There had to be something else to say, Sandie couldn't just leave it at that and move on to the next one, she was not that sort of worker, not that sort of person. "It's not nice," she continued. "None of it is nice, not any of it. Everybody tells me I have a good job and I guess I do, I can't complain about the pay, it's evenings and nights mostly but I get extra for that, and even the smell I sort of got used to after the first six weeks or so. And I'm doing something that might make things a little better for some of you. Because of what I'm doing they might catch an outbreak in time to do something. I know it's only because of the profits really that they hire people like me, it costs them if they lose animals before they can be harvested, but to me it's different, I *am* helping too, I know that. It's just that I can't, that one person can't . . ." She paused again. "I'm sorry," she said, and then she had to move on.

Broderick, many years later

LET ME INTERRUPT here once again, this time to try to give you a fuller sense than does the story being told in these pages of the physical reality of these sorts of operations. Sandie would have been one of more than two hundred employees at Canfield Incorporated. A working chattel population of at least 6,500—the number Canfield typically had at any one time—would usually require many more employees than that, perhaps even twice as many; this was one of the most efficient operations in the entire Western and Midwestern region. What Sam would have been able to see when he looked through the big gate in the morning was only a small part of it. There were over a dozen sets of pens, with each set including at least one finishing pen, as well as several pens for chattels-in-use. Around each set were barriers, just like those that Sam would have looked at every day around his own pen. Each of them was roughly three yards high and went down into the ground almost as far. No creature could climb it, no creature could burrow beneath it. On the sides that faced outward toward the rest of the world, nothing was visible. One of the core principles of any chattel farm was to keep prying eyes away, to keep outsiders out.

On the inside, every operation was a world unto itself. The crowding was standard, you'd find pretty much the same thing inside pens at any operation, it was all according to plan, but any responsible operation would place an upper limit on density. If chattels were confined at a ratio of at least three hundred to the half acre, but no more than three hundred and fifty, the operation could be financially viable and the animals would have sufficient space that most of them would not exhibit symptoms of any of the most extreme or disruptive behaviors. (Industry representatives sometimes complained at the use of the term *mental illness*, which of course had been coined for humans rather than chattels or mongrels, but you could hardly deny that they had organs inside their heads, and that things happened inside those organs.) Ergonomics and kinetics experts were consulted in establishing the optimal size for the pens to be used for chattels-in-use, and even more so for the final finishing pens. You couldn't avoid some health issues, of course; some health risk was a necessary externality if you were going to run an efficient operation, and for efficiency there had to be strict limits on how much space you gave the chattels. The important thing at every stage was that the creatures bulk up at the maximum rate consistent with the stage of production; obviously the bulk-up rate was much higher in their final months in the finishing pens than would be appropriate when they were chattels-in-use working every day in the fields, in which case no one could afford for them to be carrying around *too* much extra fat.

In the pens both for chattels-in-use and for final finishing the creatures slept in stacked rows of what would have been called bunks had they been intended for human use. They were referred to as *flats*, and flat they were, just thin sheets of steel-reinforced aluminum; there was no need for mattresses or the sort of associated creature comforts that humans have grown used to. The flats were stacked five levels high, spaced around the perimeter and, as necessary, in rows within the enclosed area. Each flat snapped onto the wall of the perimeter (or onto the retaining wall in the case of flats stacked within the enclosed area) at a half yard distance from those above and below. Beside each flat was a cube that would dispense three times per day a precisely measured amount of purée into a detachable plastic trough—one sort of purée for the chattels-in-use, another for those in the final finishing pens.

Though in some operations the compounds were floored with concrete, most were still a simple earth base. Always, though, the excreting areas had concrete floors, and always they would be grated. The chattels would stand or squat over the grate for the operation of their eliminative functions. Not everything went through the grating, and no means of clean up was provided; the chattels were obliged to wipe their hands and their anuses as well as they could at one of the standpipes that stood at each end of the grate.

Clothing, which was generally of extreme simplicity for chattels-in-use, was of course abandoned at the final finishing stage. A number of studies conducted soon after intensive chattel production began to become established had indicated that in the circumstances necessitated by this final stage, clothing was not only irrelevant and unnecessary, but indeed served as a breeding ground for infection and disease. In the pens for the chattels-in-use, the problem of infection and disease was not quite so acute as it was in the final finishing pens; theirs was a roomier, healthier environment, at least in relative terms. It was always in the final finishing pens that things were the worst. As they approached harvesting, when the important thing was not to let them move around too much, there was obviously no way to avoid having the chattels spend all their time in the muck. Inevitably, disease rates were higher: that was the price that had to be paid.

When the animals had reached their last few days in the final finishing pens, their bodies were so different from those in the chattels-in-use pens as to suggest an entirely different species. Fat was everywhere; it sagged and surged from every body. The closer the chattels were to harvesting, the more they slumped, the more slowly they moved.*

---

*In the old days age-to-weight ratios for mongrels had been very similar to what they were for humans. For, say, a nine-year-old (boy or girl, it made little difference at that age) the average weight would be about seventy pounds. But as soon as the intensive systems of chattel farming started to fall into place, all that began to change, and change rapidly. The "right" food, the "right" additives—hormones, especially—brought real results. A more scientific diet meant not just helping the creatures put on pounds, but helping them put on pounds in the right places, the areas where the cuts of meat would be most juicy—or most lucrative, at any rate. It did come down to dollars per pound, there could be no avoiding that fundamental fact. Within just five years of the introduction of intensive systems the average weight of a nine-year-old chattel was up by over 40 percent. (The effect of the innovations of the chattel industry could be clearly seen through a comparison with mongrels kept as pets, which showed virtually no change in age-to-weight ratio over the same period.) Within six or seven more years, the figure was up a further 40 percent; in barely a dozen years, in other words, the average weight had roughly doubled. A nine-year-old chattel nearing the end of its time in the finishing pens would typically weigh out at just over 140 pounds. And nine years old, it was discovered, was precisely the prime age. Even if some of them were extraordinarily productive as chattels-in-use, it would only very rarely make good economic sense to keep them around for the years nine through twelve, when the potential for additional weight gain leveled off significantly. In a truly exceptional case, one might be singled out and not sent to the finishing pens until it was eleven or twelve.

For all the years they had been chattels-in-use it would of course have served no one's interest to have them fat and slow and lumpy. The feed mix given to chattels-in-use, economical though it might be, had enough nutrients in it to keep muscle strength up to the required levels. It was only in the ninth year, with transfer to the finishing pens, that the feed mix changed and the trigger for rapid finishing was touched.

Did the finishing process really have a significant impact on taste, as the meat producers would always claim it did? Today, of course, it is no longer only the better-off who are able to express an educated opinion on such a question. The return of cheap meat has meant that a much higher percentage of the entire population may now become meat eaters again—but at what cost? And it seems clear that the average person is no different from the well-off in this respect. What matters is not what sort of creatures are hidden away in those pens or how they are treated; what matters is that what comes out of the pens and the processing plants and goes into their mouths is cheap and bland and softly palatable.* Few feel they need to know anything beyond that. Few *want* to know anything beyond that. Indeed, as I believe I touched on earlier, many will actively resist having such knowledge made available to them.† I don't know if I

---

*As a long-time opponent of the cruelties of intensive farming, I am hardly a disinterested party here, but to my mind the matter of taste is clear. Much as the producers may add to the bulk of the flesh, they do not add to its taste. The taste of a chattel that has been bulked up in a finishing pen is far blander than that of one that has spent its life entirely in the fields—and that makes it *less* palatable, not more so. Of course there is a large subjective element to such preferences, and it is clear that for the present I am in a minority; there is no shortage of demand for the bland succulence so characteristic of the flesh of today's feed-lot-finished chattel. Even on those rare occasions when conditions in the finishing pens are reported in the media—the bloated bodies, the stench of urine and feces, the diseases kept at bay only by lacing the meat with antibiotics—most people still report a preference for the flesh that comes out of such conditions over the flesh of any free-range animal. And sadly, many among the minority who do express some concern tend to be far more troubled by the effect it all might have on their own health than by the effect such conditions most certainly have on the health of the animals themselves.

†In theory, of course, everyone supports freedom of speech. But ask people what they think of advertisements sponsored by People Advocating Fair Treatment for Animals that show how chattels destined to go between our lips and our teeth are treated in the intensive farms. Not only do many people not want to look at such

have the stomach to say any more than that on a topic that I—well, by this time you know where I stand. I will try to confine the rest of what I have to say to description, and let the facts speak for themselves.

Except in the warmest and driest of climates, intensive chattel operations almost always include sleeping sheds adjacent to the outdoor pens. (In the case of Canfield's these stood to the north of the pens, not far from the rendering operation.) The practicality of having such shelter available in case of excessive cold or precipitation was obvious. But as a number of studies had shown, that high-density level made the sheds a more fertile breeding ground for disease than the pens. Inevitably, there were also temperature control problems in the sheds. The relative lack of heat in winter was not a great problem, as the bodies of the chattels themselves would help to ameliorate all but the most extreme cold. On a very warm day, however, the heat would become trapped within the metal exterior of the sheds, and the atmosphere could become stiflingly uncomfortable—sufficiently so as to put at risk the frailer animals. It was no wonder, then, that the sheds were used only in case of real necessity.

At this time of the year in a part of the world such as that in which Canfield's was located, there was surely no such necessity. Day after day the sun shone down from a blue sky; the managers could breathe a sigh of relief, as this was one of the most important periods for the crops, which meant of course one of the periods of highest demand for the chattels-in-use. Most of them now were being put to use in the orchards that lined the valley to the south of the pens. A smaller number worked the vast

---

advertisements, they think such advertisements should be banned outright. Try to tell them that the seescreen providers and the companies that own the billboards often refuse to accept advertisements of this sort, and ask them if that seems fair to them. "I don't have a problem with it," they will say, meaning they don't have a problem with denying perfectly legal not-for-profit groups such as PAFTA any way of getting their message out publicly. "I don't see why we should have to have that stuff rammed down our throats." That's the expression which is almost always used in such circumstances—"rammed down our throats." If people were to reflect a moment, they might notice inconsistencies here. You don't hear anyone saying that putting a good-looking woman in an advertisement is the equivalent of ramming her down your throat. Or that filling seescreen advertisements with luxury goods that most of us can't afford is the equivalent of ramming those expensive goods down our throats.

vegetable fields to the west. For much of the year this would be the area of highest concentration for chattels-in-use work: weeding, lettuce picking, and carrying out a number of other tasks that would be synchronized with more time-sensitive work, fruit picking of course being the most time sensitive of all. The huge tomato fields and the adjacent tomato hothouses required the attention of dozens of chattels at almost any time; during peak periods that number rose into the hundreds. At this time of year in any of these areas, a chattel-in-use might be worked for as many as twelve, fourteen, even fifteen or sixteen hours over the course of a day. But that was exceptional. For the bulk of the year the workday was unlikely to be much beyond twelve hours.

The picture would not be complete without some mention of the chattel nursery, at Canfield's located to the east of the main pens. The life of a chattel was dominated by work after the age of three, but chattels were allowed a good deal of time for play in their first two or three years—much as human children are. To some extent that entailed additional expense, expense that some shortsighted business interests would always argue was excessive. But a number of studies indicated that in fact chattels-in-use performed better later in life if this sort of early investment had been made. And, given that the bulk of the labor involved in providing for the under-threes could be performed by chattels-in-use, the "investment" was less than it might have seemed—more a matter of opportunity cost for the labor of the chattels-in-use assigned to the nursery than it was of actual expenditure.

Understandably enough, the goal of keeping disruptions to a minimum remained a priority of producers throughout the lifespan of the chattel. It was kept very much in mind in the preparation of foodstuffs, both for chattels-in-use and for those at the final finishing stage. And inexpensive but highly effective pharmaceutical products had been developed to help keep disruptive inclinations to a minimum. Even then, the authorities would always remain alert to the threat of possible disruptive activity. The story of Sam is a case in point here. As I have throughout, I will let the storyteller tell that story. But before it draws to a close I should say something more about its teller.

As a good many of you will no doubt have guessed by now, the Naomi of these pages is Naomi Okun, the renowned novelist and professor of creative writing, who began to make her name in fiction even while she was still practicing medicine. Her reputation as a novelist, of course, has been based very largely on her skill with the very sort of shifting third-person narrative—those who don't like it call it "slippery"—that she offers here in recounting the story of Sam, and of the formative years of her own life. It's a period of that now-famous life about which she has always been reticent, and which has been the subject of much speculation. I may say that it was with considerable trepidation that she allowed me to make it public in this limited and informal way, for a select group of individuals interested in exploring the issue of chattel welfare. Unless and until Professor Okun decides that she would like to take the further step of publishing the manuscript during her own lifetime, it must remain a private manuscript to which access has been permitted in this context only.

When Naomi and I first met she had almost completed the present manuscript, which I gather she had originally ventured on more as a matter of bibliotherapy than as something that might fall in the mainstream of her works of fiction—and that might find the same sort of audience. Regardless, I understand that she had carried out a good deal of research: long conversations with her parents and with numerous others, as well as an exhaustive search through family papers. Understandably enough, her focus was primarily on her own family, but it occurred to her as she neared completion of the project to try to look up the surviving members of Sam's original family. This was not all that many years ago; I myself was already becoming better known outside the legal community than within it. The name *Broderick Clark* was not spoken quite as often then as it is perhaps now in the same breath as the phrase *chattel welfare,* or indeed the phrase *chattel-rights advocate,* but it would be false modesty to deny that I was becoming well-known. It was surely not difficult for Naomi to find me.

I may say that we hit it off immediately. And I should say as well that, much as we are so different in personality and in our approach to the story recounted in these pages, I have not inconsiderable admiration for the freewheeling approach she takes. I do have some doubts and reservations. For one thing, I wonder if she may in some cases have succumbed to a temptation that I'm sure operates in all of us—the temptation to imagine that others' minds work far more in the way our own does than is actually the case. And I wonder too if in one particular respect the author may be misrepresenting herself; surely the young Naomi she imagines as the story draws to a close is in some ways too young. Does the Naomi of the final pages you are about to read—almost a teenager by this time—not seem implausibly childlike? Seem still to be too much like the younger child she was when she first met Sam? But perhaps most of us always imagine ourselves to have changed less over time than has in fact been the case. And in fairness, I have no reason to believe there exists any version of this story closer to the truth than the one Naomi tells. Whatever the flaws in its telling, it remains, I believe, a remarkable tale.

• •

When her father told Naomi what had happened she knew they would have to be moving, moving ever so fast to find him. They would find him, she knew they would, she just knew. Daddy would be able to do anything now, he did not always need to be doing what Carrie said anymore. Naomi told God that he had to fix things, he had to make sure Sam would stay wherever he was until they could find him, he would be okay.

Carrie had told Daddy how to find the house and her daddy had told Carrie no, she didn't need to come with them, first he had said that she didn't need to come, then that she shouldn't come, her father said Carrie should just say the directions to the place. Daddy was suddenly a little bit like Carrie was when she was not so nice. They should be a big family, her and Mommy and Daddy and Sammy too, and nice to each other, Naomi felt for a powerful moment, they should not be like this. She was reaching the age when so many humans are first and perhaps most strongly aware of how human life will never be as it should, but when it is never clear what will be done with that knowledge.

Naomi tried not to see Sam's little face, to shut out everything except what she and her father would have to do, where they would have to go. First, to that house. God knew where Sammy had been taken to from there, and where he was now, but Carrie didn't know that, and she couldn't tell them what she didn't know.

The Greeley Road was what Route 61 was called once it got inside city limits. Nobody was much interested in traveling to Greeley anymore, that town had pretty well dried up, and in fact nobody took Route 61 much on this side of town for any reason, the big stores and shopping malls you might want to visit were all on the south side, and anyone really wanting to go anywhere this direction would get onto the freeway from the John Street connector, they wouldn't be out here on 61. But it wasn't all run-down warehouses and vacant lots. A lot of the snooty folks uptown forgot that people still *lived* out this way. Maybe not as many as had lived here once, certainly not as many as there'd been before that one year the river burst its banks and flooded the flats and it had gotten so tough to get insurance, just about impossible, really. But Naomi didn't know any of that and Zayne didn't think any of that as he drove along the Greeley Road, it seemed so long but that was just how the time passed in his mind, in fact he found the place a lot faster than Carrie had done that night in the rain. If anything it looked more bedraggled in the light, the soffit boards on one side coming away from the eaves and the paint all faded and peeling. It looked as if once it had been some sort of turquoise but now the wood was a color more like the blue of the sky on a hazy, washed-out summer's day. An aluminum screen door banged a little in the light breeze, something most likely wrong with the catch.

"Hello!" Zayne said, and then "hello!" again when no one came to the door. Naomi could just hear his voice from the car, he had told her she had to stay in the car. Maybe nothing would happen, maybe nobody would be there. But then Naomi could see a man with a huge body that was a little bit twisted come to the door. She thought he was saying he didn't know anything, they must be confused, but it looked as if her father wouldn't let him close the door. Her daddy was pretty big and he stuck his foot in the door and the big man opened it again, all red in the face, yelling, and then Zayne was yelling too and saying he would call the police. But then he started talking differently, the twisted man did, he wasn't yelling anymore and Naomi couldn't hear what he said but finally she could hear a little bit, "There is a place just off the Woodstock Road, maybe a mile after the old Clinton

Hotel, you turn left, you go maybe two miles, it's Township Road 12. I don't know anything about any of this, you hear, but if a person like me were to know someone who knows someone who might know where to take a pet in a situation like what you say, one that was a stray, like, I'm thinking maybe that farm, maybe Canfield's is the name of it, maybe that might be the place. Hypothetically, like I'm saying, I'm not saying any more than that. And I never said that neither, if anybody asks." Then he managed to jerk the door free and Naomi's father couldn't keep his foot there anymore and it was shut and it was locked and then they were off again and that was where they went, to the place just as the man had said.

Naomi's father said as they drove he thought a man like that could be lying, how could you be sure? He said it was hard to know what the truth of it was, and Naomi believed that too, and he said it was possible Sam wouldn't be where the man had said, but Naomi didn't believe him about that part, Sam would be there, that was what she knew.

They took the roads just as the man had said, the crumbly old Clinton Hotel was just beyond the last subdivision, it used to be the center of a little hamlet, Zayne knew about the history of it, horse-drawn coaches would stop there for the night, that was very, very long ago and then all the other buildings in the hamlet had crumbled just as the hotel looked like it was crumbling now but now the different houses were creeping close to it again, and it had a new sign, LIVE MUSIC NIGHTLY, and Naomi remembered for a fleeting second how when she had seen signs like that when she was younger she had wondered how you could live music, and what it would mean to do that every night, she had never quite been able to puzzle it through. And yet at that age it had seemed natural that people would live happily ever after; those things never needed puzzling through when you were younger, it is all so different once you start to be more grown-up.

The Woodstock Road curved and dipped after you passed the hotel, and the cornfields began, this wasn't the good corn, the corn that you would have on the cob at the table, it was the feed corn, her biology teacher had told Naomi once about the difference, lower quality, tougher, not as sweet, it was corn they ground up for chattel feed but this year it wasn't looking very good, the leaves and even a lot of the stalks were turning brown, of course there had been so little rain, everyone said it. And then when they came to the Township Road 12 sign they turned, but there was no sign of a feedlot or any other business, just a break in the cornfields and a gravel road, no one would know to turn here if they hadn't been told.

And then it got dusty, very dusty, Naomi had to roll up her window so as not to let the dust fill the car, they would be there in just a minute, just a minute and they would be there. Sam would be there, he would have to be there, how could he not be there? Maybe if she crossed her fingers and held them ever so tightly it would help just a little.

And then the cornfields stopped and then it was just as the man had said, Canfield Incorporated, just where he had said but with big signs all over saying NO TRESPASSING, and high fences. In just a few places you could see through a little bit, just glimpses, you could see chattels in the muck but that was only where the fence cover was loose or torn a little bit. Mostly the cover was strung right along on the inside of the wire mesh of that fence so you couldn't see anything, only smell, it was like the bathroom when nobody has flushed for a long time, only worse than that.

There was one entrance road, it had no gate but another sign, ENTER ON COMPANY BUSINESS ONLY, and that's what they did and they found the office right near where you drove in. There was a small veranda and then a door and then when they opened that they found a woman behind a desk, Naomi thought she was maybe her mother's age, but the lines in her face went all differently, and Zayne started to explain everything about the confusion, as he called it, and could they tell him and his daughter if Sam had been admitted there a few weeks ago, dark hair, slightly built even for a child, the mongrel identification code on his left ear. But before Zayne could finish the woman had already started to say "I'm sorry, I don't think I can help you," or something like that, and the door opened behind her and a man in a shiny jacket with a bulgy face said to her that she didn't have to say she was sorry. He said it was nobody's business anyway to come snooping around there, if people lost their pet mongrels it was their own fault, there was no liability, none, did they understand that?

"Mr. Givens," the woman began as she turned to him, "these people aren't—" But the man wasn't listening to her, he was staring at Zayne, *Let me handle this, Rose*, were the words starting to form in his mind, but it was Naomi who spoke first.

"But it wasn't Sam's fault, he couldn't help it!" Her father looked at her when she said that, with a little bit of his *I love you* look and a little bit of his *be quiet* look. It was the man in the shiny jacket who replied.

"*Sam*? Listen, little girl, let's say this little one of yours really was brought here. Thing is, we wouldn't know anything about that." He was trying on a smile now, but there was aggression even in his kindness. "We take in a chattel, we don't hear no name. We take in a thousand chattels, you think they have names? That identity marker you see on every ankle, you better believe that's all the ID it needs."

Zayne could see and Naomi could see too that there was little more they could do right there and then. For a moment Zayne thought that his daughter's tears might accomplish what a simple request could not. As she began to rock back and forth the woman behind the counter slowly rose. Her high heels gave an odd lilt to her very considerable bulk as she swayed over to Mr. Givens's side. "Maybe we could let them look," she said, almost in a stage whisper, as if she wanted the father and his daughter to hear that she had kind thoughts, to make it clear that Givens and his sort were responsible for all of it. Sometimes Rose had thought through the future in her own mind, one future anyways, one way things might go. *I always tried to do what I could to help, to make things better for the animals*, that was what she would say if things ever turned against them, turned against this whole industry. *I really did try*, Rose would say, and that's what even now she believed in her heart of hearts, and maybe she was right, maybe she was trying, maybe she was a human being as good as it was possible for that human to be, it wasn't so good to always be judging, Naomi had already learned that.

Givens did not answer her, did not seem to have heard her. Maybe he really hadn't heard her or maybe his mind had gone elsewhere, you had to have a mind that could go elsewhere to work in a place like that, even more to rise to where Givens had risen to, he was management now, not management for Slyson itself, that was all out of head office, of course, but management for this one location, Canfield Incorporated, the name was in the small print on the sign that had SLYSON FOODS: TASTE YOU CAN COUNT ON in big letters.* A manager for Slyson Foods itself need never see how the animals were treated—or how the farm workers were treated, for that matter. But a manager at an operation such as Canfield, that was a different thing. Admittedly, you didn't have to have all the horror right in front of you all the time, you could stay in your office a lot and you need never work the flesh-cutting blades or the gutting machines for the blood processors, but you had to *know* it all, all the way through. You'd get inured to it to some extent, sure, you'd have to, but at some level it was always there, in a place where no amount of euphemism could expunge it.

"We'll keep trying, we'll keep coming back, there has to be some way," Zayne told Naomi as he cradled her shoulders and they walked away.

And they did come again. Zayne did not mean to, at first, he thought it might be too painful for her, he thought there was no hope, maybe he had always been a man who gave up too easily. But Naomi made him come back. He could not say no to her and maybe that was

---

*[Broderick Clark's note] Standard procedure was that the running of each farm would be contracted out to local operators. Slyson wouldn't own the land, sometimes wouldn't own any of the animals either, but they'd have the exclusive right to buy the animals at a certain price—a price that the independent operator would have little say in. Slyson would have control over the whole process; the local operator would have to buy the feed they specified, and everything had to be built to specified dimensions. The time the chattels spent in the finishing pens had to be standard too. It all followed the same sort of model that had been developed before the great extinctions by the big companies. Slyson had been one of them, and Premium Grade had been another (later becoming America's Pride). ConFarm, Fargill, and Farmland's Finest were the others; each had used the contract method to expand the size of its empire. To expand its profitability too, for under the sorts of contracts they developed, the big producers both then and now found ways to insulate themselves from almost every risk; it was the small local operators who bore the risks. (I say "small" even though many of them processed thousands and thousands of animals per month; small they nevertheless were by the standards of the larger companies, and of the industry as a whole.)

as it should be, there are some times when parents should never say no to their children, Zayne knew that. Carrie knew that too: when Naomi asked her one night when her father was busy on his big, dark painting and saying *No, not tonight*, she went to Carrie, they had not touched each other at all since the night that they never spoke of now, but Carrie hugged her and said *Yes, yes* she would go with Gnome, and Naomi shrank away from her only a little. The two of them went together but it was no better that night than the others.

They kept coming in the darkness, though, sometimes Naomi and her father, sometimes Naomi and Carrie, and once all three of them, they would creep up together to the high fences of chain metal with the green coverings tied all along the inside, and they would follow along until they came to the places where there were tears in the fabric, where the wind had rucked up a corner, anywhere there might be a place to peer inside. But there was never any sign of Sam, no sign at all when they peered in, nothing except the dark shapes of nearly naked bodies, hunched, slumped, sprawled on their flats, dozens upon dozens upon dozens of them, dirty and smelly and always wide-eyed, fearful whenever they saw the eyes that were seeing them through the fence. The creatures would sometimes mumble at them in their confusion and fear, "Sop grl, sop grl," one of them said what sounded like that to Naomi, was it *sop* or *soft* or maybe *stop*, did it want her to stop looking at them?

Sometimes they would stay silent and just look, other times they would call out again and again, low but insistent, "We are looking for Sam. He can talk but he cannot hear. We are looking for Sam," Naomi would say again and again, and two or three times they thought they heard a voice answering, perhaps it was the same voice each time, but it was not Sam's voice. "Ot ere, ot ere." No, not there. The other times there were no words, no answer, nothing, only the grunts and sighs of sleep, and always the smell.

Carl turned the animal round, keeping its forelimbs high. "This one's not been here long, you say?" "No, just a few days." That was Curtis. There were just three of them on duty in the Special Processing

Unit that morning; Brandon had called in sick. "Still at the classification and processing stage. Apparently it's been living as a mongrel its whole life. I make it maybe eight now, maybe nine. Guess whoever it was decided they didn't need a pet around the house any longer!"

"So what's the routine with one like this? Just throw it in the pen with all the seven- and eight-year-olds?"

"Dunno. You know, Eddie?" Eddie Mellor had been at Canfield a long time. Neither Carl nor Curtis knew for sure, but Carl thought maybe neither of them had even been born when Eddie had started.

"It'll be heading for the finishing pens straight away, I guess. Try to fatten it up a bit, and that's that. Not our decision to make." He looked at the torso of the creature in front of them. "One look at it you'll see it never got fixed when it was little. They don't always do that when they're mongrels. A lot of the owners think they want to keep them natural-like. Me, I'd think better to make sure it stays real docile, make sure it's not going to cause no trouble. Anyway, there's no question we want them docile, eh Curtis?"

"You better believe it. With you in charge there's not gonna be any chattel revolt. Besides, if a chattel hasn't been done it'll always fetch a worse price. Cut them off or cut your profits. Everyone knows it changes the taste of the meat, and not in a good way, you know, if a thing hasn't been done."

"Yeah, that's what they always say. I wonder where they get the meat to compare, these days. Even those free-range operations have them done, that's what I hear." Eddie chuckled in a jangly sort of way. "Anyway, I'll be happy to take it on faith." He paused a moment more. "Let's get 'er done then, eh?"

When a chattel came into the system late like this one had, there was no "assembly line" castration as there was for the yearlings born into a chattel farm. Of necessity an older one like this would be given individual treatment, with two or three hands taking it through the procedure in the Special Processing Unit.

"Clamp it to the apparatus first—do that before it gets the injection, 'cause it's the injection even more than the procedure that you need to keep it still for. I sure ain't no doctor, and finding a vein, hitting it just right is a lot harder than finding what's between the legs of the thing, I can tell you that!"

"Yeah, right," Curtis put in. "So with the injection it can't feel anything?"

"I don't know about that. From the way they squeal and twitch around you have to think they feel it. And you wouldn't want it so's they couldn't walk around at all afterward, so's we'd have to lug the thing back to the pen ourselves. But a jab of this stuff takes away some of the feeling, no doubt about that, makes them sluggish-like. And the big thing is what it does to the blood, helps to stanch the flow, you know. We put a high-quality bandage on the affected area too, disinfectant, the works. But it helps if the blood's been thickened a little, I guess, helps the thing to scab over."

"Was it like this in the old days with steers and them? You used to do them too when you started, didn't you?"

"I been doing this a lot of years, you got that right. Yeah, I guess it was—really, it's been so long now. The setup's quite a bit different, of course, the restraints and all for a four-legged . . . With a steer, now, we used to restrain the head between the bars of the feeders. We used to use that and a tail-hold, you'd just grip and hold, putting a bit of pressure on, upward and forward." He paused, reflecting; for all the years he'd been in the business, this was not a comparison he had often contemplated.* "But yeah, sure, I guess it's the same principle

---

*[Broderick Clark's note] As it turned out, Mellor would have occasion to contemplate such comparisons a good deal more thoroughly. When the Senate convened its special hearings just a few years later (this was to look into all aspects of the chattel industry in response to concerns as to the humaneness of the practices followed), Eddie Mellor was among the witnesses; he and three other old-timers were called to give first-hand testimony comparing the treatment of chattels in the early twenty-second century with the treatment of cattle in the mid twenty-first.

The transcript of Mellor's full testimony is available in the government archives. It runs to some forty-four pages. The excerpt below is from that part of Mellor's testimony that bears directly on this point in the current narrative. Readers should be warned in advance of the explicitness and the crudeness of the testimony.

With the steers there were a number of ways to go—not just surgical castration like we do with chattels. With a chattel you don't have the

as in the old days. Same result, too!" The three of them laughed. But a small voice inside, a voice stilled through long force of habit, knew that the shivering little creature that they now held down on the table would be able to feel everything they were doing to it. And the voice told them that it was wrong.

"Jesus, this one's really shaking. Give it a little more of that . . . Give it another injection, will you?"

Eddie stopped himself. He had been on the point of saying, *What are you, going soft?* Instead, he found a syringe and, without saying a word, started feeling for a vein.

Sam could feel the fingers prodding and poking, and then the needle brushing against his skin, just below the elbow. He couldn't stop the shivering, he was so tired, tired of all the feeling, couldn't there be no feeling? Please make the needle take away the feeling,

---

option of the bloodless methods, the old burdizzo or the elastrators, a chattel'd be able to just take those things right off. Just big elastic bands they were, really, put those suckers round the scrotum and then you just wait till it falls off." [Laughter in the committee room.] "Okay, you think I'm joking, but that's how it used to be, anyone who worked on a farm back then'd tell you. Take about three weeks for the things to fall off, generally. Thing was, you'd think that sort of method'd be safer and kinder too. We never gave the steers no shots, no painkillers, nothing. But the more research they did, the more they said that the surgical method hurt the critters less in the long run, and was safer too. The other way, see, you'd get a lot of infections. The surgery, you do it right and it's done. People used to think we'd lop off the whole thing, scrotum, balls, the works. But that part we'd do just like we do it now with a chattel. Just cut off the lower part of the scrotal sac, the last third maybe. Then slip the testicles out until you see them dangling by the sperm cord, and then you take one of 'em and you keep on pulling, slow and steady like, they say that makes the blood vessels tear in a way that gives you less bleeding. A bit of snipping to get those last bits of tissue, then same thing with the other one, and you're done. With a chattel we spray on some antiseptic but we never did that with a steer. Never that much bleeding if it's done right. Or with an older one you'd maybe use the emasculators, they'd do both testicles at once after you'd opened up the scrotum, crush them first to make for easier removal. But we don't use those with chattels. I don't know as how they've developed tools that would work just right. Everything's so small with chattels, that's the thing.

make it make there be no feeling.

He felt none of the special horror that would have come with knowing beforehand exactly what they were about to do to him. If he had known they were about to cut him—if he had known *where* they were about to cut him—maybe he would have been panicked, screaming, pissing himself. And maybe if he had been trying to he could have read their lips the whole time, figured out most of what they were saying to one another, maybe almost all of it. But somehow just then he had not wanted to try to read anyone's lips. When you know things ahead of time it makes it worse sometimes, because so often they are bad things, almost always, really. Sam looked up at the ceiling, it was all splotched and dark, he felt the needle go in now, the pressure easing as it slipped past the nerves into where he could not feel, and then the room was disappearing in some strange way, as if it were being drained of itself, and then he thought he felt something sharp very far away, and then he could not feel, there was nothing to feel.

Rose ate at home that night with her husband, Jesse, just the two of them, just like they did just about every other night of the year. Some people might have found it boring but what was the point of spending all your hard-earned money in restaurants? A lot of couples, you'd see them there, they'd be paying half a day's wage to have a steak dinner at the Country Kitchen out toward Lakeview but they didn't really seem to be enjoying it, they'd just sit there and look at each other or past each other at the curtains or the knickknacks on the plate rail or the trucks going by down Highway 61. She and Jesse, they weren't like that, they had gotten along pretty well to start with and they got along even better now that the kids were grown and off on their own, a lot of people they'd look at each other when the kids grew up and think, *I don't know that person across from me*, or even, *I don't know that person across from me, and I have no particular desire to get to know them.* With Jesse and her it had been different, oh sure, sometimes they wouldn't talk to each other too much, sometimes Jesse'd have the seescreen on full volume right through dinner, he said he liked to keep up with the news and Rose didn't much like that, she'd asked him a thousand times not to, why couldn't he read the paper or run the thing at a different time, you could find out that stuff on the seescreen any hour any which way, but most of the time it was pretty good, the kids might think the two of them were too old to fool around now but they weren't, better to spend your time like that going to bed a bit early than sitting in the Country Kitchen, that was for sure, and Jesse and her could talk, they could talk about anything, they could and they did, just this week Jesse had kept telling her how he worried over what would happen to Rose when he was gone, he was older, Jesse was, he still worked at the depot and he had no pension, neither did Rose, and he worried about it all and Rose loved him for that but there wasn't any answer, was there? You just had to keep on living and see what happened. She told him then about the man with his little girl that had come into the office, you didn't see something like that every day, really, Givens should be a little less quick to show people the door, that was what Rose thought, and then for some reason she said, "You know, Jesse, sometimes I wonder about some of the stuff we do out there, sometimes I think it wouldn't hurt us to not eat any of that stuff ourselves, I don't mean just cut down on the fatty bits, I mean any of it, I know that sounds crazy and sure we get the staff rates, it's not that pricey for us but still, sometimes I wonder if it's not good, what we're doing to the animals and all, sometimes I think it's just wrong, maybe it wouldn't hurt us to cut back on it at least," strictly speaking it wasn't true to say *sometimes I wonder*, that made it seem a little like she might have been thinking this way on and off for a while, considering it all from this angle, that angle, when in fact the idea had just popped into her head right then for the first time.

They would talk about it a bit that night, and a bit more a few nights later, and then six months after that Jesse said to her, "You know, I've been thinking a bit about that stuff you brought up about the animals and all, it's starting to get to me a little too," in fact what was starting to get to him a little was not precisely a worry about the animals themselves and the way they were treated, it was vaguer than that, more distant, like a worry that he *should* perhaps worry about such things more than he had been doing, which was to say not at all. But that was indeed a significant change. We often imagine that if people change their views on some important issue they go through a process that involves a good deal of pondering about the thing directly, nagging doubts appearing, conscience gnawing away, that sort of thing. And that can happen, sometimes that does happen, and sometimes there's a blinding flash of realization like what happened to a lot of people more than a century ago when they read what the philosopher Peter Singer had written about animals, but just as often change happens as it was with Rose and Jesse, ideas popping up as if from out of the blue, vague worries that you should be concerned about something you haven't in fact been concerned about, and then maybe months or even years and years go by and suddenly you can come to realize that you hold in your mind, already fully formed, a conviction that the way you had been used to seeing things all that time ago had been wrong, of course it had been wrong, any sensible person could see that you had to do x and not y. That was how it was with Rose and Jesse. Eight, nine years later Rose told Jesse out of the blue that she'd decided she should stop cooking meat, stop eating the stuff, and Jesse said yeah, they should go that route, for sure most of the time they should and it turned out that most of the time was all of the time and they never missed it, it never even seemed important. The thing about the pension was important but it turned out that Jesse was able to work into his eighties, just light work, mind, but still it brought in a few dollars and Rose's wage was pretty good, she kept working too, they died within a month of each other. You can see the memorial stone the kids arranged to have placed in the graveyard up on Cemetery Hill. They never said anything about a stone, they were cremated, but Danny and Christine and Tom, all of them thought there should be something with their names on it, the Country Kitchen they never went to is down below by the highway, the lights start to twinkle every evening as the sun goes down and the trucks roll past, most times that's how change happens and things carry on.

* * *

Naomi knew that her father and Carrie too were thinking they should give up. They weren't saying so, but that was because they wanted to save her feelings, Naomi was pretty sure of that. What they *really* thought was that Sam was gone forever. And they were so wrong about that. Sam could be found, she knew he could be found. And that's what they would do. She hated it, though, hated the darkness when there was no moon and they could hardly see anything, they had to just peer forward anyway in the darkness and call out softly, and she hated that any second somebody might see them, one of the keepers. They were breaking the law, she knew that, but they were in the right, really. The law didn't always follow what was right, Naomi knew that from learning in history class of the old laws about slavery and about women, but it was another thing to know it like this.

Sam was in there, she knew he must be in there, why wouldn't anyone answer and tell them, couldn't anyone?

Within days of the procedure Sam had been transferred to one of the special pens, the pens reserved for chattels that were considered to be disruptive. Mostly they were aggressive ones, females who happened to have a lot of testosterone or males that emasculation hadn't made docile enough, that was what the textbooks said, anyway. You couldn't say Sam had been aggressive—no scuffles, no pushing or shoving even. But there was something about him; he kept mumbling to himself, and to the other chattels too, they weren't likely to understand anything and he didn't make any sense anyway, everybody knew that. But still. *Just to be on the safe side*, that was how Givens had put it.

Givens was right—that much should be admitted straightaway. If they had let Sam stay in with the others he might well have become what they would have called disruptive. Something had changed in Sam, maybe it had been happening for a long time inside him. For almost all his short life he had accepted everything that had been done to him. And, more widely, he had accepted everything that happened as being simply the way things do happen. He had been almost entirely without the reflex or the impulse that prompts the clenched fist, the blotched face, the cry *It's not fair!* But now, from somewhere deep inside him welled up a feeling that it was *not* fair, that this should not be the way things happened. These were creatures like him, all of them, not like him exactly, maybe not all could think or speak as well as he could, and for sure they would never be able to build skyscrapers or write books, books like the books Naomi used to show him how to read *how he missed her how he missed her how he missed her*, these were not humans, they were mongrels—*chattels*, if you had to call them that—but he was living among them and he was thinking they were not so very different, certainly not so very much worse. Not worse than him, not worse than other humans, either. All those special things that a few humans can do, humans would hold up those things to try to show that they were somehow better, all of them. Except they weren't better, not most of them, most of them didn't do any of these things, Sam knew that, and even the ones that did amazing things were often nasty to strangers, friends, even their families. And for the most part creatures that were human just ate and slept and worked and sometimes they made themselves stupid with drink and stumbled around and got happier or nastier, or both, and beyond that they never did much, most of them. It was no good to pretend that you were higher, better, you'd never be able to keep the things apart, you'd always just end up thinking you were better than all the other creatures, you'd always end up thinking it was all right to do anything to them, let anything happen to them, let them be used any old way, let them be killed, let them be eaten, eat them yourself, kill them and eat them even when you had no need. All around him he could see how the others that they called chattels could feel the same pain that he felt, could feel fear, in their way could feel love and be loved, the things that he could feel. All this was wrong. And it would not be made right if Sam were treated as a human, a deaf human, and not as a chattel. He could see all that clearly now. He was not so young, really, not anymore.

There was a window in the huge dark building behind the pens, a single window, and always there was light behind it, and pink and red hunks of meat gliding by, on some sort of conveyor hoist it must be, red oozing from the flesh, it must be right near where the line began. Even if you woke and looked up in the middle of the night, always it was there. Sam knew there was a line, he had heard about this from Sandie a little bit, and a little bit he had watched the lips of some of the men keepers, he knew that when you went in there your body would be caught by hooks and swung upside down. But you would be knocked out by the stun gun, and maybe you wouldn't feel much, maybe you would feel nothing and the knife would slice across your neck and that would be that, but you might be twitching, and there was always some movement until the blood ran out. Toward the beginning of the line you were almost whole, then the limbs were gone, the guts, after that there would still be something on the hook, one large chunk on its hook on the line, still something that could be called your remains, and then not anything recognizable as part of a creature. The hunks that would become steaks would be taken and trimmed separately as the remains were carried on mechanically, the rolled roasts, chuck roasts, and so on—it was a scraggly thing that would be taken off the line for final processing, the grinding, rendering, and everything that was done with all the little extras salvaged along the way. It was better not to look up at the window, not ever.

"Thel kill u, u no. Thay will, thel kill me too. Thel kill al of us." That was the sort of thing Sam said now to many of the others. He was not panicky, he was hardly scared even, these were just facts they should know, was it wrong to try to warn them? It was something terrible that they could do nothing about, something that would happen to them anyway no matter what he said, maybe it was not right to scare them like this, was he scaring any of them? He did not know, but something inside him said that he should try to warn them, warn them even if they could do nothing to stop it. Mostly they did not seem to know what he was saying, and then he would point with his index finger at the side of his head, and again as if with a blade to the throat. They did not understand him, the chattels, most of them anyway; maybe the one he called Josh, though, he was pretty sure Josh understood a little bit at first, maybe more than a little bit. Josh had flinched when he had heard Sam say those things and make those motions to two or three of the others, and then when Sam had tried to tell him too he had wrapped his arms round his neck and

Sammy knew it was better not to say anything, not just now, so even Josh maybe never really understood what Sam had been saying, not fully. But the ones that ran things, the Canfield workers, *they* heard the noises, they saw the hand motions, it was the hand motions above all that made them say to each other *We can't leave him out there; the special pens, that's where he should be.*

No animal stayed long in the special pens. As soon as you reached the minimum weight at which slaughter could be economic, that was the end of it. Sam had not been long in the main pens before his transfer; now the end would come more quickly. He knew as soon as they put him in the dark pen, six foot by three foot, gray concrete all around, a feeding trough at one end, a metal grate for his waste at the other, he knew as soon as they put him in there that this was the last place. He had had a little life and some of it had been a good life and he had had his mother in it and he had had Naomi in it and they were there in his heart to make it warm. And he knew that now he did not want it to keep going on and on.

From the first day in the special pens he refused to put his hands to the food in the trough, not even for a moment to touch it, the chunks or the gooey slops. It was two or three days before the keepers began to sense that anything might be wrong. Of course they thought first of illness and disease, of germs and parasites, either way the result would be the same. If the animal was not adding weight, it was not adding value. Give it some antibiotics and cull it immediately was the normal procedure. It would be grade B meat, but get the problem out of here, that was the main thing. A special tag to identify the grade of meat would go on it, you had to keep the grades separate. Tuesday evening was the next time in the schedule for doing specials on the line.

It was over between Carrie and him, Zayne thought. He reckoned it had effectively been over the night she had told them what had happened, the true version of what had happened. But perhaps even before that—now he could not be sure precisely when the thread had begun to unravel. In any event, the unraveling could not now be stopped, of that he was sure, as sure as he could be sure of anything.

But so often it is impossible to tell what will happen between people. So often we think it will be impossible for a spark to be struck between two people, and then it is. So often we think it is all over between people and then something happens, people change, and none of it is as we had expected. Zayne was wrong, as it turned out. It was not over between Carrie and him, not exactly. To be sure, there would be years of mistrust, years of distance, and starting a few months after it had all gone wrong they would live in separate homes, only a block or two away from each other, but separate. That was how it would go and how you might think it would have stayed, nothing between them but history, and distance, and sharp words and feelings. But over the years the mistrust started to wear away, and all the things that had been rough and sharp between them—the pushing and pulling that in the end was perhaps over no more than power itself, the issues over their daughter—all that too began to wear away, like sandstone, until there was nothing very distinctive about how they got on with each other, but what there was had a smooth surface to it, nothing sharp, and nothing underneath that might erupt. Sandstone. Nothing strong enough to last a thousand years, but none of us are here for a thousand years; for humans sandstone is strong enough. Perhaps you could not call what came to exist in the space between them *love*, but it was more than indifference, it was more than the fact of a shared daughter and the desperate need they both felt to help her heal and to grow into her own life. It was more than any of that, though it would have been hard for either Carrie or Zayne to put a name to what it was or to how much of anything it was. But they saw each other almost every day; often Zayne would linger in Carrie's kitchen over coffee, and once or twice a year one of them might have a few glasses of wine more than they had planned after dropping by. At a family dinner or over the holidays one might say to the other, "You know, we weren't that bad for each other," and the other would agree and might add, "and we aren't that bad for each other now." Once or twice a year they might end up making love, and one time, it might have been two or three years after Sam had gone out of their lives, one of them decided to stop eating meat. It was only a couple of months before the other came to the same decision. And years and years later they would both decide—again, quite independently—to put each other into their wills; almost everything would go to Naomi, of course, but each left a few things of meaning to the other.

It was too much for her to keep going back to Canfield, Zayne saw that, they would have to stop these outings, she had made him promise to take her one last time but this really would be the last. After that they would just have to hope and pray, he knew no god but he could hope, and she had the strong bitter faith of the young person who is on the point of leaving youth behind. Naomi could pray for both of them.

They do the specials at night, that's the policy at most every farm. The minders and keepers have their prods when they lead the animals out of the pen, if they veer off one way or another you'll feel it. Not too many volts, just enough to jolt them back into line. Mostly the whole thing is nothing more than a job for the keepers, but sometimes it has a little more meaning. It was like that for Jenson, a drifter that Givens had hired the month before. Jenson loved to use the prod, to feel it in his palm and see what it did, see how they jerked and yelped when he touched them with its charge. Three, four times he touched the very fat one ahead of Sam as they herded all those who were to be culled that day from the special pens out into the main holding pen. Then into the approach path, one by one. The one ahead of Sam must have somehow sensed what was happening, he turned and started to run, "Sto, sto, sto," he was crying, it was pathetic really, one so much above weight, how could he think he could get anywhere? One of the keepers caught up to him before he was more than a few yards out of the line, pushed him so he staggered and fell forward into the muck, and then Jenkins gave him the prod, again, again, again, until Ferguson, who was in charge nights but had stayed on after his shift ended that morning, told him *Enough, we're here to get a job done, right*, g*et him back in there*, and they pushed him back into line, now three or four back of Sam.

The path went in rows back and forth, back and forth, as it moved forward, with high dividers between each row so the animals could not see the end of the line but only knew it, knew how it was getting closer, could feel the vibrations and hear the *pop, pop, pop* of the stun gun.

Sam did not feel scared, he felt empty, he had a knowing of death inside him now, he would be all right, he told himself that again and again and again, *All right all right, it's over, all right all right*, he kept saying the words as he shuffled forward. And then he thought of other words, of words tumbling over one another, of stretching words, of words shuffling forward. He thought back to the beginning, to when she had taught him the thing words, so he could ask for *cracker* and talk about *turtle* and *toenail* and *water* and *earth* and *sky.* And then *hungry* and *thirsty* and the doing words, *pushing* and *grunting* and *thinking*, all those were there for him now. And the words were not from the world only, the words that were in him now. They were *the mole had been working very hard all the morning, spring-cleaning his little house* and *Alice was beginning to get very tired of sitting by her sister on the bank, and of having nothing to do* and *here is Edward Bear, coming down stairs now, bump, bump, bump, on the back of his head, behind Christopher Robin.* And from the words, from her lips as the words came from the books, he had learned *afraid* and *sadness* and *despair.* And *lonely*, Sam knew *Max the king of all wild things was lonely*, and he knew *lonely* from within himself. And he knew Josh must know those things too, and all the others must know them, not from the words or the books but from the feelings, *water* and *earth* and *sky*, *hungry* and *thirsty* and *lonely*, *pushing* and *grunting* and even in their own way *thinking*, but he had been so lucky, Sam had, somehow so lucky really. And the luck that he had found for that short time when he had learned from the words and from everything—he had learned *love* too—was a strong warm thing inside him.

The wild things had roared their terrible roars and gnashed their terrible teeth but Max had said *Be still!* and then, when once more the wild things had roared their terrible roars and gnashed their terrible teeth, *Was it like that behind the window don't think don't think don't see don't see*, they had loved him so but Max had said no, had sailed back and in and out of weeks and into the night of his very own room.

The path narrowed at the end to a ramp, fenced each side, narrow, narrow, the knocker always wore a rubber apron, huge gloves, safety goggles, a man had to protect his eyes, if the stun gun were jostled, or if an elbow caught his eye as the body was yanked up and away by the pull chains on the hoist conveyor, or if something went wrong with what the sticker was doing just a few feet away as the sticker made the first cut, the cut that should sever the blood vessels in the neck, something could slip, sometimes the knife was dull and the cut didn't go deep enough, not the first one, and the sticker would have to have a second go at it, but other times it was too sharp and the sticker was maybe a bit off balance or something else would make the blade go clear through the spine. And of course the blood, there was none of that from the stun gun but from where the sticker worked the blood went everywhere, drenched everything, so you had to wear protection, a hardhat, good safety goggles, thick gloves, Ellison wore protection on his arms too, not everyone did when they were working as a knocker but Ellison thought it was prudent, he was just doing this for the summer, that's what he was thinking anyway, by the end of the summer he could stop, he would've saved a bit, saved enough so that Shelley and him could rent a bigger place, a two-bedroom maybe.

"Daddy, look way over, look way over Daddy, I think it's him." It had been so long, it felt so very long, since her voice had held such feeling inside it. They peered through the ripped fabric, it was perhaps thirty yards away that the ramp sloped up into the square opening, the jaws of the building opening bright, stray screams cut short by the stun gun, the bodies in their sudden softness jerked up, "Not there, no, do you see? On the path, see? in that line," that was where Naomi thought she could see him, at the end of one of the rows as they turned, "Wait, he'll come by again, I know it's him, the binoculars, quick quick, you have them I know you do, you can see it's him, you can see it is, it's Sam," she called, and then again "Sam, Sam," forgetting after all this time that he could not hear, forgetting everything until her father shushed her, threw down the binoculars, smothered her almost, it was warm suddenly but dark, so very dark.

"No sweetie, it isn't him, really it isn't. I know how you wish we could find him. I know. But it isn't him." Zayne stopped. What could he say? There was nothing to make it go away. The word *lucky* came to him, came out like sudden horror. "Lucky, lucky this time. We would not want it to be him."

"No, no, it mustn't be him." Naomi's voice was hushed now, she had gone all quiet. *But the others*, she thought, *the others, all those other ones.*

How could he have told her? No one could have told such a thing to a young—no, she was not a young woman, she was still a child. It would have been too late anyway, surely it would have been too late, wouldn't it? From that far away, how could they have done anything to stop it? And if he had tried, if he had stood up and started to shout, if he had somehow gotten their attention, the ones over there on the killing line, would it have done any good? Of course not, of course nothing would have changed, nothing would have stopped, but the damage, the damage to the child, to his daughter, there had been so much done already, how could he do more now? No, it was better to have said nothing. But what of the other child? Suddenly he thought of Sam, and tears covered his face. He was shaking. *It's okay Daddy, Daddy it's all right, I know I wanted it to be him, I wanted it so much to be able to save him and it isn't him and you're so sorry, and Daddy I'm so sorry, let me be the sorry one, those ones are going to be killed they have been killed now, and he isn't one of them, it wasn't Sam, Daddy, we can go home now Daddy, now Daddy we can go, now, Daddy.*

* * *

A two-bedroom maybe, Ellison thought, it would be important to have a bit more space now that there were going to be three of them. A bit more money too, he had saved a bit here and there, maybe he could go back to that clothing store if they'd have him, the pay wasn't quite as good but anyway he wouldn't stay here beyond the fall, that would be the end for him, what was that sound, like someone crying out, not the gibberish of the animals. Some human sound, a child it almost sounded like, *same, same, same* was it calling? No, nothing could be calling, there was nothing out there, nothing could be out there this time of the evening, he pressed the tip to the next skull, the eyes looked at him as if in another place already, with most of them you could see if you looked that they had seen what was coming and you could see how much it scared them, it was better not to look but if you did you could see what they saw, and in the next moment there was pleading in their eyes, he hated that, but this one was so calm in its eyes, so gentle almost, the way someone looks if they love you, love you not for you only, but just for being like anybody else. You could imagine so many things if you looked in a creature's eyes, you could never know, it was like looking into clouds, or into water, you could never know really, it was better to look away. The night was cold, suddenly very cold, and still such a long line, still such a very long line.

Author's Afterword

Let me begin this afterword by imagining an extension to the text of the novel itself, a paragraph that would carry the story forward in a different direction:

> Two or three years after Sam had gone out of their lives both Zayne and Carrie stopped eating meat. But the first change in their habits came immediately; they stopped eating all the products of factory farming. And they were not the only ones. Even before the full measure of their grief had taken hold—if they had waited even a day or two it might have ended up undone forever—they phoned a friend who worked as a stringer for the *Times*. And suddenly the story was everywhere, *I never really knew*, people said, *I had no idea it was that bad*. And because most people are not evil if evil is shown to them in a form that they cannot look away from, there was all of a sudden broad agreement that things had to change. Within weeks the industry had adopted voluntary guidelines for improved treatment of livestock; within months governments at all levels had brought in comprehensive new regulations making such practices mandatory even for factory-farming operations, toughening cruelty-to-animal legislation and amending it to apply as fully to feedlots as it did to the treatment of pets. Some governments went even further, ensuring that the small operators who had traditionally been the most humane were given the means to compete with larger ones. Within a very few years the overwhelming majority of people had decided that they were more than willing to pay a bit more for peace of mind, for the knowledge that

the creatures they were eating had been humanely treated before being killed. Truly free-range products became the norm rather than the exception, and meat eating in general declined markedly. Five years after Sam's death there were features in almost all the major media on the mongrel whose death had brought about a revolution.

To what extent would this constitute a happy ending to the novel? Quite aside from the question of the fate of Sam, Josh, and the others, most human animals today would argue that no ending in the dystopic world of *Animals* could be "happy" if it stopped short of a general renunciation by the entire populace of the practice of eating yurn.

But what of a happy ending outside the confines of this novel—in the real world of the early twenty-first century, not in an imagined world of the early twenty-second? Much of the point for me of creating Sam as the being that he is in the circumstances that he faces was to inquire into the particular reality for a sentient creature much like most of us: what would it be like to face something akin to today's factory farming? No doubt a novel of this sort will provide fodder for philosophical debate on the wider arguments concerning whether or not humans should kill and eat non-human animals; indeed, I hope it does. But the most urgent topic for debate and for action today is not that one; it is the issue of factory farming. Let us not forget the large philosophical questions. But let us focus above all on the 99 percent of cases about which almost all humans in possession of the facts are likely to agree—not the 1 percent over which there is likely to be lively argument for the foreseeable future. In today's world more than 99 percent of farm animals (I refer here to dairy cattle and laying hens as well as to animals raised to become meat) lead the lives of utter misery that factory farming demands of them. On the desirability of bringing such misery to an end surely all readers can agree, once they are in full possession of the facts.

But what are the facts? The suffering that Sam is subjected to in the last part of this novel is so extreme that it may well seem implausible to some readers. Surely no innocent creature capable of feeling could legally be made to endure such suffering, or not at least in any society even remotely like our own. Yet every day both in North America (where this story is set) and around the world millions and millions of cows, pigs, and chickens endure far worse than this. When they are branded, when their ears or their beaks are mutilated, when they are castrated, no anesthetic is used. When they are slaughtered they are often still conscious as they begin to be bled, skinned, and sliced open. The conditions in which they are forced to live—those of pigs and chickens and dairy cattle even more than those of beef cattle—are considerably worse than those that Sam and Josh and the others endure. Kept in pens in which they are often unable to turn around, such animals lead lives of unutterable misery. They are bred and raised using methods designed purely to facilitate the production of cheaper and cheaper flesh, eggs, and milk for humans to consume, and those methods typically make them unnaturally proportioned and make their bodies function in unnatural ways—almost always to their considerable pain and discomfort.

None of this is a secret; all of it has been going on for decades; the first edition of Peter Singer's *Animal Liberation*, which drew so many people's attention for the first time to the cruelties of factory farming, appeared in 1975. It is true that none of it is widely or frequently reported in the mainstream media. And it is true that the atrocities are generally carried out far from prying eyes, behind high fences or in closed sheds or pens. But the information as to what goes on remains widely available. Those who would like more evidence may easily find it in abundance in print and on video.

Why, then, do we allow it to continue? If such things were being done to cats and dogs (or to wolves or giraffes or grizzly bears), they would be considered serious criminal offenses and the human perpetrators would be given substantial prison sentences. But somewhere we draw a line, separating one sort of animal from another. On our side of that line are pets and wild animals; on the other side of that line are beings against which we allow virtually any cruelty to be inflicted. We give our children picture books that show such animals living out their lives in happy pastures—and that often personify them, give them human names, show them talking to one another.

But in practice we do not treat the *actual* animals as living beings, as beings who may not be capable of speech but who can feel pain, and feel a good many other things too. We treat them purely as food, as things it doesn't matter how we mistreat, as things to be eaten, as things to be tortured if that will make the milk and flesh and eggs cheaper or tastier.

In most American jurisdictions animal-cruelty legislation as it pertains to farm animals is either toothless or nonexistent (though the passage of Proposition 2 in California in 2008, putting some limits on cruelty to animals in some factory-farming situations, is a hopeful sign). In Canada the Liberal government of 1993 to 2005 failed three times to enact even watered-down animal-cruelty legislation, and the subsequent Conservative government shows no desire even to attempt to try again. In much of Europe and Africa things are considerably better than that, but in much of Asia and South America they are considerably worse.

What can be done? Pressing governments for change should not be given up as a lost cause. Writing letters to the editor can have an impact, as can e-mailing or phoning in one's opinions to radio and television programs. Talking up such things among one's friends and relatives can be helpful too. But probably the biggest single thing we can do to help bring change is simply change our own habits.

For those of us who may be considering such a change for the first time, it is important to recognize that it need not be an all-or-nothing thing. Many who have thought about these things and who are not comfortable supporting the cruelties of factory farming nevertheless continue to do so because they cannot readily see themselves changing their entire lives, and they imagine that to do anything they would have to do everything, would have to change their entire lifestyle. Some may argue that anything short of a totally vegan diet is an inadequate response, and certainly people who are inspired to make that sort of revolutionary change in their lives in one dramatic step are to be commended. But most recognize too that any improvement is a step in the right direction. Anything is far, far better than nothing, and things may be done in a series of small steps. That's something I can attest to personally. I was persuaded many years ago (largely through reading Singer's book) to give up factory-farmed meat, chicken, milk, and eggs, but I continued for many years to eat the "happy meat" of non-factory-farmed animals, and to consume their eggs and milk too. Four years ago I gave up all meat, and was pleasantly surprised to find it not at all difficult to do. A couple of years ago I did the same with all seafood except shellfish. Soymilk has now mostly replaced cow's milk in my diet, but I still eat some dairy products from non-factory-farmed cows and goats. Increasingly I am persuaded that many shellfish are more susceptible to pain than I would like to think, and that I should eliminate shrimp from my diet. By the time I turn sixty (in another four years), I may well be a vegan, and a part of me would like to become one now, but I have to acknowledge that for me, slow stages seem to represent what is achievable. And I know that those slow stages are a good deal better than nothing.

Once we begin to act—at whatever pace we can—we will no longer be tempted to avert our eyes from the effects our actions have on thousands of other living, breathing, feeling beings. This is true, I should emphasize, regardless of our particular beliefs as to what it means to be human, as to what sort of line may separate human beings from other beings, or as to precisely where that line should be drawn. This novel has to some extent explored those issues, and may have often seemed to be blurring any line between human and non-human. It has not done so with the intent of arguing that the distinction between human and nonhuman is without meaning. It has done so, rather, with two purposes in mind. The first is to lead readers to question that other, much more deadly line that society draws between animals that deserve our respect and good will (wild animals and pets), and animals that we permit to be subjected to tortuous lives before we eat them. The second is to make it possible more fully to imagine the lives of non-human animals, and more fully to sympathize with their plight. Those who posit a clear dividing line between human and non-human have often suggested that one uniquely human quality is the power to exercise a moral imagination: the power to imagine ourselves in the place of another being, and to modify or change our own actions in the light of that imaginative experience. Whether or not such a quality is indeed the unique preserve of humans I do not know. But if we fail to put such imaginative power to use—and if we fail to take action to right wrongs when we realize the effects our actions are having on others—then we are helping to sustain a system founded on almost limitless human cruelty.

ACKNOWLEDGMENTS

In many ways this book has been a collaborative effort. Along the way I have received gentle criticisms and helpful advice from a considerable number of people, and as a result of their comments this book is in a great many ways better than it would have been had I worked in isolation. I would like to thank in particular Barbara Berson, Elizabeth Brake, Marc Ereshefsky, Chris Griffin, Bruce Henry, Martha Hunter, Thomas Hurka, Jackie Kaiser, Naomi LePan, Ann Levey, Melanie Little, Anne McWhir, Mical Moser, Maureen Okun, Denise Oswald, David Regan, Deborah Robbins, P. K. Page, Kathryn Shevelow, Peter Singer, Andrew Steinmetz, and Angus Taylor.

I would like to also acknowledge the influence of two individuals who did not read or comment on the manuscript in advance of publication—but who have been instrumental in shaping the way I now think about the issues dealt with in these pages: Tammy Roberts and Melanie Safka.